NONNA MARIA

and the Case of the Lost Treasure

NONNA MARIA

MARIA

and the Case of the Lost Treasure

A NOVEL

LORENZO CARCATERRA

BANTAM BOOKS
New York

Published in the United States by Bantam Books, an imprint
of Random House, a division of Penguin Random House LLC,
New York.

BANTAM & B colophon is a registered trademark
of Penguin Random House LLC.

Library of Congress Cataloging-in-Publication Data

Names: Carcaterra, Lorenzo, author.
Title: Nonna Maria and the case of the lost treasure: a novel / Lorenzo Carcaterra.
Description: First edition. | New York: Bantam Dell, 2024.
Identifiers: LCCN 2023029687 (print) | LCCN 2023029688 (ebook) |
ISBN 9780593499214 (hardcover) | ISBN 9780593499221 (ebook)
Subjects: LCGFT: Cozy mysteries. | Action and adventure fiction. | Novels.
Classification: LCC PS3553.A653 N65 2024 (print) | LCC PS3553.A653 (ebook) |
DDC 813/.54—dc23/eng/20230626
LC record available at lccn.loc.gov/2023029687
LC ebook record available at lccn.loc.gov/2023029688

Printed in Canada on acid-free paper

randomhousebooks.com

2 4 6 8 9 7 5 3 1

First Edition

Book design by Fritz Metsch

This one is for my three Italian aunts—Francesca, Anna, and Nancy.

I will never forget their love and kindness, their amazing meals, and the many hours of laughter.

Their memory will never fade.

NONNA MARIA

and the Case of the Lost Treasure

1.

THE MAN PULLED a chair from a small outdoor table and sat down. He stared out at the busy port of the Italian island of Ischia, watching as fishermen unloaded their morning catch and tour boat crews washed and scrubbed upper and lower decks, anticipating yet another busy day in what was proving to be a busy summer season. A young waiter walked over to the table and smiled at the man. "The pastries are still in the oven," he said. "Should be out in a few minutes. But the coffee is fresh and ready to pour."

"Coffee's all I need," the man said. "Double espresso. Stronger the better."

"Sounds like you're in need of a wake-up call," the young waiter said, still holding the smile.

The man turned his attention away from the port and glared at the young waiter, his eyes the color of stone. "I'm in need of a coffee," he said. "Nothing more."

"I didn't mean to offend you," the young waiter said, losing the smile. "I was merely trying to make conversation."

"That's something else I don't need or want," the man said. "Just bring the coffee."

The young waiter rushed toward the entrance of the café

3

while the man reached a thick hand into the side pocket of his white jacket and pulled out a butane lighter and a small cigar. He sat back, popped open the lighter, and watched as the flame flickered across the front and sides of the cigar. He then put the cigar to his mouth, lit the rich, charcoal-colored tobacco, and let the thin lines of smoke filter up around his face.

He was in his late forties, with an angular and handsome face marred only by a thin scar just below his lower lip. He wore loose-fitting clothes—a designer jacket over a black crewneck shirt, light gray cargo pants, and black sandals—though not loose enough to fully hide the muscular chest and forearms resting beneath them. But they did hide the revolvers holstered on each hip.

His name was Maurizio Carnale, and he had come to Ischia not for the thermal waters nor for the great beaches, the abundant sunshine, or the top-tier restaurants.

Maurizio Carnale had come to Ischia for only one purpose. To kill a man. And when it came to the art of murder, there were few better to be found in all of Europe than the man sitting at an outdoor café on a quiet summer morning waiting impatiently for a double espresso.

2.

NONNA MARIA SAT in a wicker chair, a warm cup of espresso resting on a side table, two of her granddaughters sitting on soft pillows at her feet. She was dressed in widow's black as she had been every day since the death of her husband, Gabriel, many years ago; and her thick white hair was folded in a bun held in place by a handful of long, thick pins.

"Nonna, tell us the story of the Greek giant who made Ischia from a large rock," the older of the two granddaughters, Isabella, said.

"I've told you that story many times, little one," Nonna Maria said. "You should know it better than I do by now."

"I do know the story, Nonna," Isabella said. "And I've tried to tell it to Concetta, but she doesn't believe me, and she asks too many questions. And I don't know the answers to all of them. Not like you."

Nonna Maria rested a hand on top of Concetta's head and smiled down at the dark-haired eight-year-old. "It's not a story to be believed," she said. "It's a story to be passed down. From me to you and to Isabella. And then, one day, many years from now, from you to your own children and grandchildren. That's what makes it a special story."

Concetta rested her head against one of Nonna Maria's legs. She was two weeks shy of her ninth birthday and was as curious as a kitten. "Did your mother tell you the story when you were my age?" she asked.

"She did," Nonna Maria said. "Many times. And I loved hearing her tell it. She was a great storyteller, my mother, and listening to her, sitting as close to her as you are to me, made me feel as if we were the only two people in the world and that she was letting me in on a secret only the two of us would share."

"You see," Isabella said to her sister, "I told you it was a special story. But when I say it, you pretend not to listen."

"You don't tell stories the way Nonna does," Concetta said. "You make them sound silly. Nonna makes them sound real."

"You know what makes a good story sound even better?" Nonna Maria asked, pushing her wicker chair back and heading toward the kitchen.

"What?" Concetta asked.

"A cup of hot cocoa and two slices of fresh bread with Nutella," Nonna Maria said.

Nonna Maria believed, as did many her age living on the island, that a hot drink was the ideal way to keep a body cool on a warm summer day.

"I like the story already, Nonna," Concetta said. "And you haven't even told it to us yet."

3.

"THE GREEK GOD Zeus was angry," Nonna Maria said. She was pacing around her kitchen table, Isabella and Concetta sitting on wooden chairs, two empty cups and two small plates tinged with crumbs and smears of Nutella resting by their elbows. "A giant had come down from the mountains and demanded three pots of gold he said belonged to him. If Zeus refused, the giant would cause the ocean to rise and kill the people who lived close to the shore."

"What did the giant look like?" Concetta asked.

Nonna Maria stopped pacing and looked at her granddaughter. "He was bigger than the tallest building you've ever seen," she said. "And strong enough to pull a dozen trees from the ground with one hand. His skin was green and lined with scars. His eyes were the size of plates and the color of mud. He had a loud and fierce voice, and his words were filled with anger. Throughout the land he was feared by everyone who crossed his path. Everyone but Zeus."

"Why wasn't Zeus scared of him?" Concetta asked.

"Zeus was the ruler of the land, and he had sworn to protect his people against any enemy," Nonna Maria said. "He had fought in many wars and defeated all who stood in his way. He was more than a Greek god. He was a warrior."

"Was he strong enough to beat the giant?" Concetta asked.

"Stop asking questions," Isabella said, "and let Nonna tell us the story."

Nonna Maria rested a hand on Concetta's shoulder and smiled. "It's good to ask questions, Isabella," she said. "You've heard me tell the story many times before. This is the first time Concetta is hearing it from me. She doesn't know the tale as well as you do. Be patient with your sister."

"Did you ask your mother many questions when she first told you the story, Nonna?" Concetta asked.

Isabella shook her head and cupped her face with both hands. "It never ends," she said.

"I asked my mother many questions, Concetta," Nonna Maria said. "My mother was a patient woman, and she answered every one. But much like Isabella, she probably wished I had asked fewer. In time, as I heard the story over and over, I learned to listen more and save my questions for when she finished telling the tale. And I have no doubt you will one day do the same."

"So, did Zeus and the giant get into a fight?" Concetta asked.

"Yes, they did," Nonna Maria said. "It was a battle that went on for several days. Neither the giant nor the god was willing to surrender. They fought on land and then moved to the sea, the waves in their wake so large they crashed against the highest mountains. Houses trembled, people of the towns ran for any shelter they could find, animals scattered into the hills."

"Did they fight with their hands, or did they have weapons?" Concetta asked.

"Both," Nonna Maria said. "The giant tossed large rocks and boulders at Zeus and the god would send bolts of lightning from his fingers into the chest and back of the giant. The force would buckle his legs, but with the courage of a lion and the strength of a bull, he would shake off the pain and charge Zeus, looking to drag the god down into the depths of the ocean."

"But a god can't lose a fight, Nonna," Isabella said. "No matter how big or strong his opponent."

"Anyone can lose a fight, Isabella," Nonna Maria said. "Even a god can be brought down."

"So, Zeus lost to the giant?" Concetta asked.

Nonna Maria looked at both her granddaughters and shook her head. "No," she said. "Not this time. Zeus came roaring up out of the deep water and with all the strength he had, he brought the giant to his knees. He rained blows on the giant, slammed boulders on top of his back, and pulled trees from the earth and smashed them over his head. The attack lasted for three days, and then the giant finally fell face down to the ground, defeated."

"Was he still alive?" Concetta asked.

Nonna Maria nodded. "The fight had been taken out of him," she said, "but he lived. And now it was left to the god to punish him."

"Did he send the giant to prison?" Concetta asked.

"No," Nonna Maria said. "Zeus knew no prison could hold such a powerful man. Instead, Zeus lifted the giant onto his back and carried him across the oceans and the seas until he

9

reached these shores. Then he brought him to the very bottom of the bay and held him in place, his back, neck, legs, and head squeezed into the soft dirt. Zeus then reached for the largest boulder he could find and rested it on top of the giant's chest. And there the giant stayed, buried under that boulder for two hundred years."

"And that's how Zeus killed him?" Concetta asked.

"This giant couldn't be killed," Nonna Maria said. "He could only be stopped. After living under the waters of the bay for two centuries, with that massive boulder on top of his chest, the giant began to move. He woke from his deep sleep and regained his strength. He then wrapped his hands around the boulder and squeezed the rock as hard as any rock could be squeezed. Slowly, over long periods of time, large pieces of the boulder came up to the surface and one by one they formed an island. This island. The island of Ischia."

"The giant made Ischia?" Concetta said. Her voice was filled with excitement and her eyes were opened wide in surprise, with the unspoken beauty of a child being told a story that amazes.

"He did," Nonna Maria said. "Over many years, the giant molded the large boulder. He began with the highest point—Mount Epomeo—and worked his way toward Forio and Serrara Fontana until he finally stopped at Ischia Ponte and the castle."

"And was he able to free himself from the boulder?" Concetta asked.

"No, he wasn't," Nonna Maria said. "He still lives under the waters of our bay. Even with all the pieces of the boulder he used to make the island, it was still too heavy for him to lift it off his body."

"There are places on the island that are named after the

giant," Isabella said. "To let us know where he is, and which parts of him we are walking on. Isn't that right, Nonna?"

"Panza, which as you know means stomach, is one place," Nonna Maria said. "That's on one end of the island, and Testaccio, which means head, is on the other side. And remember the earthquake we had here a few summers ago?"

Isabella and Concetta both nodded. "Did he make that happen, Nonna?" Isabella asked.

"You see, you have questions too, and you've heard the story a lot more times than I have," Concetta said to her sister.

"This is a part I didn't know," Isabella said. "Nonna never told me."

"He might have, but he probably didn't mean for an earthquake to happen," Nonna Maria said. "He was trying to get the rest of the boulder off his body. That caused the land above him to shake and some of the houses to collapse."

"So, the giant is not our friend," Isabella said.

"He wants to be free, Isabella," Nonna Maria said. "Like everyone else. And in his attempt to free himself, he left us with a beautiful island."

"I really wish I could visit him, Nonna," Concetta said. "He must be so lonely after all these years. He built our island, but he never got to see it."

"I'm sure he can see it, little one," Nonna Maria said. "Even from the bottom of the bay."

"But he won't ever be able to go home again," Isabella said. "Back to Greece. Back to his family. He'll always be here. Buried under the island."

"He is home," Nonna Maria said. "He built this island with his own hands out of a rock that was meant to keep him a prisoner for eternity. It belongs as much to him as it does to the people who have lived and died here over many years. The giant doesn't need to go back to Greece. There is no longer a place for him there. And any family he might have had has been gone for a good many years. We are his family now."

4.

ISCHIA IS HOME to sixty-five thousand year-round residents, living within six boroughs that make up the eighteen-square-mile island. In the winter months, the residents can walk the streets in relative tranquility, and navigate the roads without concerns that tourist traffic will keep them from meeting with nearby friends and relatives.

The island was first discovered by Greek colonists centuries ago. The thermal mineral waters of the island are believed to heal conditions ranging from arthritic pains to gout to kidney and liver disease. Michelangelo was so taken with the medicinal powers of Ischia he built a home on the island. Roman generals, Julius Caesar among them, came to Ischia to mend battle wounds. In the 1950s, Truman Capote came to write and enjoy the views of the Bay of Naples from the windows of his rented villa and set a short story on the island.

As the centuries passed, Ischia became a summer gathering place for Italian movie stars and an assortment of counts and countesses. They were soon followed by a contingent of American movie stars, from Burt Lancaster to Jack Lemmon and the director Billy Wilder. The latter two were so smitten with Ischia, they filmed *Avanti!*, a 1972 feature film, on the island.

If any two celebrities can be credited for turning Ischia into a tourist destination, it would be Richard Burton and Elizabeth Taylor.

In 1962, the two fell in love while filming *Cleopatra* on the island. They began what was considered a scandalous affair, bringing paparazzi to the island by the boatload. "The photos were printed in every magazine and newspaper in the world," Roberto Affini would tell any tourist who asked how Ischia became such a popular destination. He would stand behind the counter of his children's clothing store, fold his arms, and recall the years he was a young man working a struggling business. "The photos got the attention of developers. Not long after that, hotels began to be built, new restaurants opened, and tour buses and cabs replaced the horse carriages that lined the port."

For decades it was Northern Italians, British, Australians, and Germans who flocked to the hotels and beaches. For a few summers, they were joined by Russian tourists, and then came the Americans.

The influx has had its downside as well. "As I get older, I miss the quiet years more and more," Nonna Maria would tell her nephew and doctor, Agostino. "We didn't seem to need as much back then. And what little we had, we took the time to enjoy. I don't know, nephew. Maybe it's my age catching up with me. But I miss those simpler times."

"Your age will never catch up with you, Zia," Agostino said. "I have patients decades younger, and they would have trouble keeping up with you. But you're not wrong. Simpler times are often better times."

"The island I know will always be part of me," Nonna Maria said. "That's one thing progress can't take away. I have my coffee. My wine. My friends. My family. And my memories. I can't think of anything else I need."

5.

IL PRESIDENTE LIT an unfiltered MS cigarette and inhaled, keeping the wet tip in his mouth. He stood with his back to a shuttered door, hidden away from the cluster of passing tourists and congested traffic. He ignored the blaring horn of the incoming hydrofoil, its two decks crammed with passengers and luggage, yet one more sign that the summer season was running at full throttle. Il Presidente tilted his head slightly, continuing to ignore the noise and bustle around him, and focused his gaze on the man sitting in a café sipping a cup of coffee and smoking a thin cigar, staring out at the activity surrounding him.

Il Presidente didn't know the man, had never laid eyes on Maurizio Carnale prior to this early morning, but he understood all too well why such a man had come to Ischia. There was a time when Il Presidente was such a man himself, hired to bring harm to another. He had spent decades working in the shadows, emerging from the darkness his profession required only to inflict pain, and only when he was hired to do so.

He had returned to Ischia and for far too many years lived a life of isolation and loneliness in a one-room apartment on the very edge of the harbor. It was a dilapidated hovel that was oven hot in the summer months and drenched in dampness during the bleak winter months. He was a desolate man destined to die much as he had lived—forgotten and dismissed by all.

All except for Nonna Maria.

Two seasons ago, Nonna Maria asked for Il Presidente's help, to free a friend from trouble. In return, she gave Il Presidente a place to live—the first floor of her two-story white stone house, a home that Nonna Maria had lived in since she married her beloved late husband, Gabriel, decades ago.

In return for room and meals, Il Presidente helped Nonna Maria with work around the house, tended the garden, and served as a valuable protector in the event she ever ran into more trouble than she could handle as she went about her work to help her friends.

After many years of darkness, after the shunning and shaming, Il Presidente finally had a home.

He finally had a family.

And he would do all he could to protect his family from harm.

6.

IL PRESIDENTE PULLED back a chair and sat across from Maurizio Carnale. He sat with his back to the port activity, his massive frame blocking Carnale's view of the nearby boats and shielding him from the rising rays of the sun. Carnale eased the cigar from his mouth and blew a stream of smoke toward Il Presidente. "Did it look to you like I wanted company?" he asked in a low, hoarse voice, rubbed raw by the steady barrage of cigars.

Il Presidente shrugged. "Not really," he said. "And that's not the reason I sat down. If you were looking for company, I wouldn't be the one you'd want sitting here. But I do need to talk to you. Five minutes of your time, if that."

"I was going to get a second cup of coffee," Carnale said. "If you're buying, then I'll listen. For five minutes."

Il Presidente caught the eye of a passing waiter and signaled for another round. "I don't usually see men in your line of work here on the island," he said.

Maurizio Carnale smiled. "And what kind of work is it you think I do?" he asked.

"The kind where you do someone else's bidding," Il Presidente said. "The kind where you agree that in return for an envelope filled with euros, someone will die. And it doesn't matter to you who that someone is."

"Whether that's true or not, I don't see how it's of any concern to you," Carnale said. He sat back, watching as the young waiter rested a fresh cup of coffee in front of him, placing the empty one in the center of a small tray.

"It's a concern only if the someone you wish to harm is someone I know," Il Presidente said. "Someone I care about."

"You have the look of a man who doesn't care about anyone," Carnale said. "The look of a man who once worked the same profession you claim I now work."

Il Presidente nodded. "We all have a certain look, the way we move, the way we carry ourselves," he said. "It's a look that's hard to hide. In my case, it worked to my benefit not to. People had made up their minds about me even before I stepped into my former life. And, in your case, I spotted the look the minute I saw you walk off the hydrofoil."

"Then you, more than anyone else, should understand I can't back away," Carnale said. "Once a job is accepted, it must be seen through to the end. Now, if the target is someone close to you, well, that is not my doing. As you know, we don't choose our targets. They are chosen for us."

"You're new to this island," Il Presidente said. "So you're not familiar with its ways and habits. News here is not spread from reading a newspaper or watching someone on television. It's spread quietly from one ear to another. It spreads even faster if it's about someone they know who might be in danger."

"And who do they think that someone might be?" Carnale asked.

Il Presidente smiled. "Keep in mind that up to this point it's only gossip," he said. "But you're from the North and I don't need to be told you didn't come here for the thermal treatments. Which means you are here either to bring harm to someone or help draw attention away from the one hired to complete the job."

"And you base all this on some street gossip you picked up?" Carnale asked.

Il Presidente nodded. "Street gossip here on the island," he said. "I put a bit of weight to that talk, but not much. But if the talk comes from Naples, then I give it more attention."

"You still haven't told me who you think I'm here to harm," Carnale said.

"I know whoever hired you in the North would have no reason to send you after a local," Il Presidente said. "But the head of the carabinieri stationed in Ischia comes from your end of the country. My understanding is, he was an active cop when he was stationed there, and he put a big dent in one of the crews. That, to me, would mean someone is eager to see him brought down."

"Let's pretend all that is true," Carnale said. "Why would a man like you care whether a carabiniere goes down or not?"

"That's my business," Il Presidente said. "What I came here to tell you is that on this job you need to concern yourself with more than just the assigned target. You will need to go up against me as well."

"I'm sorry to hear that," Carnale said. "But if getting the job done means taking your life, then I have no problem with that."

"Then we understand each other," Il Presidente said. "And you don't need me to tell you the risk you face going after the target."

"It wouldn't be the first time a carabiniere was marked," Carnale said. "It's happened a number of times in the past."

"If you manage to succeed, your reputation as well as your fee will grow beyond what it already is," Il Presidente said. "That's one side of the coin."

"And the other?"

"The other side is a much darker one," Il Presidente said. "You will be a hunted man, not just in Italy, but anywhere you go in Europe. Unlike the ones who work their trade in our world, those with badges never forget to bring down or bring in the man who killed one of their own. Even if you're lucky enough to live, hide from their gaze for a year, maybe two, they will never give up the hunt. And once you're caught, they will toss you inside a hole and leave you there to die. They will call it a prison sentence. But you and I both know it will be nothing less than a death sentence."

"If I was afraid of the risks, I wouldn't have taken the job," Carnale said. "You know that as well as I do. Are you sitting there ready to tell me you've never taken on a job that brought with it great risks?"

"I was never asked to do what you've been asked," Il Presidente said. "Whether you're the primary or a decoy doesn't matter. You will be judged guilty one way or the other."

"Maybe you weren't given a job like this one because the bosses didn't think you were as dangerous as you like to pretend you were," Carnale said with a slight smile, placing the cigar back into the corner of his mouth. "That is, if the talk you heard both here and in Naples is even close to the truth."

"I was as dangerous as I needed to be," Il Presidente said.

"And as dangerous as anyone you've been up against. I want to leave you with one final thought, and it is one you should burn into memory."

"Can't wait to hear it," Carnale said with a shrug.

"I will be working against you on this," Il Presidente said. "The carabinieri captain is friends with someone I am close to. Someone I owe my life to. If she were injured in any way, you will not need to fear a long prison sentence or anyone with a badge. It is me you will need to fear. It is me who will bring an end to your life."

Il Presidente stared at Carnale for a few moments. He then eased out of his chair, stood, pulled a twenty-euro bill from the front pocket of his dark jeans, and tossed it on the table. "Enjoy the coffee," he said.

He turned and quietly and slowly disappeared into the crowds now filling the area around the port.

7.

NONNA MARIA WAITED as the young woman pulled out a hard-backed chair and sat across from her, a nervous smile crossing her lips. She poured espresso into a cup and slid it across the wooden dining room table. The young woman nodded her thanks. "My grandfather always told me the strongest cup of coffee he ever had was sitting at this very table," the young woman said.

Nonna Maria nodded. "Paolino was one of my husband's best friends," she said. "The two shared many a meal together, and nothing completes a good meal better than a strong cup of coffee. I was sorry to hear of his death."

"I got to spend a great deal of time with him," the young woman said. "He was alone at the end and needed looking after. With both my mother and Nonna gone, he had no one."

"He had you, Rita," Nonna Maria said. "And that was all he wanted or needed. You want the ones you love the most around you during those final months. It's a comfort knowing they are there."

"He talked about many things during that time," Rita said. "About his life, his travels, his friends. But most of all he spoke to me about a secret he had kept to himself for all these years.

He wanted me to know. He needed me to know. It was something he wanted me to have. Something that had been kept hidden for many decades. He said I would need a great deal of help to find it and that I should come to see you. That you would be the one to help me."

"I've known you since you were an infant in your mother's arms," Nonna Maria said. "If I can help in any way, then I will."

Rita sipped her coffee and smiled. "That's exactly what Nonno told me you would say," she said. "He told me you can always be counted on to help a friend."

"Does the help you need require you to share Paolino's secret with me?" Nonna Maria asked.

"I'm afraid it does, Nonna Maria," Rita said. "And it's a secret that comes with a long history attached to it. And some danger."

Nonna Maria pushed back her chair, stood, and walked into the kitchen. "If you're going to share a secret," she said, "it's best to do it with food. I baked an apple pie earlier today and it should have cooled down enough by now for you to have a slice to go along with your second cup of coffee."

"I don't mean to be a bother to you, Nonna Maria," Rita said. "But you are the only one I trust with the secret my grandfather passed on to me."

"Having a friend eat and drink at my table is never a bother," Nonna Maria said. "Only a pleasure."

Nonna Maria stepped back into the dining room and rested a plate filled with a large slice of apple pie in front of Rita. She handed her a folded napkin and a fork and then poured her a second cup of coffee. She sat down across from Rita and watched as she cut into the pie and enjoyed her first taste. "I've always

24

heard people talk about how great a cook you are," Rita said. "And they're right in what they say. This pie is the best I've ever had."

"There's no secret to it," Nonna Maria said. "All you need is time and a good stove. That's something most old women on this island have."

Rita smiled at Nonna Maria, cutting free another sliver of pie. She was in her late twenties, slender, with shoulder-length dark hair and caramel-colored skin, browned by many summers spent under the hot Ischia sun. She had an easy manner about her, eyes filled with youthful curiosity and a contagious smile. She reminded Nonna Maria of her mother, Felice, who died when Rita was not yet ten years old. She briefly flashed on the night she sat by Felice's bedside, holding a cool cloth to her friend's forehead, dreading the moment when she would take her last breath.

Nonna Maria waited until Rita had finished eating the pie and drinking the coffee. "The rest of the pie I'll pack for you to take home," she said to Rita. "The sugar I put in my coffee is the only sweet thing I can have these days."

"Thank you," Rita said. "I'll share it with my neighbor, Raffaella. As you know, she was a big help to us during the months my grandfather was bedridden."

"Now, tell me how I can help you," Nonna Maria said.

"You know about the caves on the island," Rita said, putting down her fork and sliding her coffee cup to the side. "And how they were used down the years. Nonno said as far back as when the Nazis occupied the island during World War II."

"Goes back even further than the Nazis," Nonna Maria said. "When the Moors occupied Ischia for over two hundred years,

25

they would use the caves to store the wine they made from our grapes. And before them, the Greeks would use them to keep their grains and flour fresh."

"And in the nineteen-seventies until the mid-nineties, the cigarette boat bandits, the ones who moved contraband cigarettes, wine, and whiskey from Naples to sell to the locals used to hide both their money and goods in the caves," Rita said. "And it was also a safe haven to keep their boats away from the Coast Guard and the carabinieri who were always in search of them."

"Those cigarette boats were much too fast for the ones used by the Coast Guard and the carabinieri," Nonna Maria said. "I would see them from the Lido racing along the shoreline. They would begin their runs around sundown and not stop until the first light of morning."

"My grandfather knew the caves very well," Rita said. "He knew about the secret ways to get in and out. He knew the history, passed down to him by his father as it had been passed to him by his own. He had been going in and out of them since he was a boy, swimming to most of them from his father's fishing boat."

"He told you these stories while you nursed him during his illness?" Nonna Maria asked.

Rita nodded. "He loved talking about it," she said. "His eyes would light up like a little boy's as he told the tales of the great fortunes he had heard were hidden there. Of the battles that were fought within the passageways. And of the bodies that had been left behind, never to be discovered."

"And then he told you a story that involved him," Nonna Maria said, "and now has been passed down to you."

"Yes, Nonna Maria," Rita said. She spoke with a slight tremble in her voice. "He told me there was a treasure hidden within the walls of the caves. A lost treasure. And that treasure belonged to him and would now belong to me."

"Did he tell you what it was?" Nonna Maria asked. "And in which of the caves it was hidden?"

Rita shook her head. "He was planning to," she said. "But his mind would wander, the medicine would tire him, and he often repeated stories he had already told me. He died before he could tell me what was hidden and where it could be found."

Nonna Maria sat in silence for several moments. She glanced up, past Rita, and looked at the framed photo of her beloved husband, Gabriel. They had loved each other from the moment they met, on a side street in Ischia Ponte, and that love had only grown in their decades together, raising a large family through good times and bad. She lost him to a form of cancer she had never heard of and had worn the widow's black every day since. But in her mind, in her very soul, and within the walls of the two-story stone house they had lived in since their wedding day, he was still very much a part of her life. To Nonna Maria he was where he always had been—in her heart.

"Do you have any idea of what it could be?" Nonna Maria asked.

"No," Rita said. "But after the funeral, as I was going through his belongings, I think I found something that might be of help."

"What did you find?" Nonna Maria asked.

Rita reached into a pocket of her yellow sundress and took out a folded and worn sheet of paper. She peeled it open slowly and rested it on the center of the table.

Nonna Maria glanced down at the sheet of paper. There were

pen and pencil markings scrawled across the page, the inscribed lines faded by the passage of time, the arrows and the writing barely legible. Nonna Maria looked up from the sheet of paper and gazed across the table at Rita.

"It's a map," Nonna Maria said.

8.

CAPTAIN PAOLO MURINO was leaning against the railing on the far end of the Lido, looking out at the lights shining on the islands dotting the Bay of Naples. He was off duty but still wearing his carabinieri uniform, his hat braced under his left arm. He was in his mid-thirties, his thick brown hair kept regulation short, his body lean and solid from his daily five-kilometer early morning runs. His face was tanned but still retained the rugged look of his Northern Italian roots, highlighted by brown eyes that seldom betrayed his true thoughts. He had been stationed in Ischia for six full seasons now, making him the longest-tenured carabinieri captain to hold the position. Two summers ago, he met and fell in love with the daughter of the port's pharmacist, and they were soon engaged and made plans to marry. The marriage had been twice delayed, once due to a family illness and the second time having to do with a case Captain Murino was too deeply involved in to focus on wedding plans.

Nonna Maria walked up to Captain Murino, her ever-present large black tote bag held in her right hand. She stood next to him and gazed out at the bay, her thick white hair, the color of an early morning cloud, intermingling with the lights along the Lido and casting her in a soft glow.

"I see I'm not the only one who likes to come here late at night," she said. "It's a good way to bring an end to a long day."

"I started coming here when I first was assigned to Ischia," Captain Murino said. "I didn't have any friends back then, didn't know any of the men under my command. I would look out at the waters thinking about how I ended up here and wondering if it was indeed the place for me. There was many a night I stood here until the sun rose and it was time for me to report back to my post. This was the place that helped me fall in love with Ischia."

"The very sick man who came to warn me about the danger you will be facing," Nonna Maria said, "is he still in Naples? At the hospital?"

Captain Murino turned to glance at Nonna Maria and shook his head. "He's still in Naples," he said. "But not at the hospital. His body is at the morgue. He died yesterday afternoon."

"I'm sorry to hear that," Nonna Maria said. "I knew him for only a short time, but it was long enough for him to come warn me about the threat on your life. It was not something he needed to do. Especially in his condition."

"You were lucky, Nonna Maria," Captain Murino said. "You met him days away from the end of his life. You would not have wanted to be in his company when he was in full health."

"I can't speak for the life he may have led," Nonna Maria said. "I only saw a sick and dying man who spent his final days sending a friend of mine a warning."

Captain Murino rested both hands on Nonna Maria's shoulders, gripping them tenderly. He looked down at the old woman and smiled. She had been one of the first ones to welcome him to Ischia, and he valued her friendship and had come to count on her for help in solving cases involving the locals, most of whom were reluctant to put their faith in a carabiniere not born on the island. But more than that, he had come to think of her as family.

"You are my friend," he said to her. "The best one I have on this island or anywhere else. And I know how desperately you fight to help your friends. I not only respect you for that, I love you for it. Trust me, it's a rare quality that few can lay claim to. But with this current situation, I am asking, pleading, as your friend, to let me handle this on my own. I know the kind of people who have me in their sights as well as you know the ones on this island. I know how they think, and I know how vicious they can be. And the last thing I want to ever see happen is to have anyone bring harm to you because of me."

Nonna Maria raised a hand and held it to Captain Murino's face. "If you are in grave danger, what kind of friend would I be if I didn't try to help you any way I can?" she said. "You have your men to help protect you, and I will do nothing to get in their way. But I will be there to help you. As will some of the other friends you have made on this island. You may have come from the North, but make no mistake, Captain, you are one of us now."

"These will be dangerous men, Nonna Maria," Captain Murino said. "If they are sent here to kill me, they will not hesitate to do the same to anyone who gets in their way."

"We all have to die of something, and we all have to die someday, Captain," Nonna Maria said.

"There is no talking you out of anything you set your mind to, is there?" Captain Murino asked.

"Only one man had that ability, Captain," Nonna Maria said.

Captain Murino smiled at Nonna Maria. "Your husband," he said.

Nonna Maria nodded and returned the smile. "Yes," she said. "But in this situation, he would take my side. And yours."

Captain Murino gazed up at the bright stars overhead. "It's getting late," he said. "Would you mind if I walked you home?"

"I never mind the company of a friend," Nonna Maria said. "And while we walk, Captain, maybe you can tell me why dangerous men want you dead."

9.

PAOLO MURINO CROSSED the unlit courtyard, his weapon drawn, his eyes scanning the shuttered apartments surrounding him. He leaned against the edge of a statue of a cherub and signaled the two carabinieri crouched by the entrance of the courtyard to hold their position. "I hope you're not thinking of going in there alone." The voice coming through his earpiece was that of his commanding officer, stationed in a van parked half a block from the housing complex. "You don't know how many might be in there."

"We don't know if anyone's in there," Murino whispered into the mic attached to his leather jacket. "There are no cars or motorbikes parked in front of the building. He's got five safe units spread throughout the city. This is only one of them."

"No cars or bikes doesn't necessarily mean no people, Murino," his commander said.

"Only one way to find out," Murino said.

Murino sprinted from the cover provided by the cherub toward the thick wooden door of the apartment building at the back of the courtyard. There were six apartment numbers listed in the index box, with a buzzer assigned to each one. The space for each name was left blank. "If he's here, his apartment would be on the second floor," Murino said into his mic. "The first and third are for his security team."

"And he never travels without his security team," his commanding officer said. "If it holds to prior practice, there will be three gunmen on the first floor and three more on the third. With you in the middle. They might have cameras in place on all the floors. You'll be spotted soon as you get through the front door. Please, Murino, don't go in without backup."

"I didn't know you cared so much about me, Bruno," Murino said.

"Believe me, I don't," Bruno said. "I'm just trying to prevent another situation like we had at Santa Croce."

"I'm going in alone *because* of what happened at Santa Croce," Murino said.

Murino braced himself against the thick wooden door. He reached into the side pocket of his black leather jacket and pulled out a brown switchblade and flicked it open. He eased the tip of the blade into the keyhole and, with a series of slow movements, worked the gears of a lock that had not been changed in decades.

He pulled the blade out soon as he heard a click of the gears. He snapped the blade shut and placed the knife back in his pocket. He then put a hand around the silver cylinder in the center of the door and gave it a gentle push. The door swung open, and Murino stepped into the foyer. It was a wide space, thick old walls flecked with peeling paint and planters crammed with flowers in desperate need of watering. The hall smelled of urine and the marble floors had long ago lost their luster. Murino moved toward the circular staircase on his left and began a slow walk up the steps. He was halfway up when he heard a door creak open. He moved away from the railing, his left shoulder braced against a damp cement wall, and continued up the stairs.

He reached the landing and saw the door closest to him swing open. He pointed his gun at the door and watched an elderly woman pull an empty grocery cart into the hall. She was caught off guard, and before she could react, Murino pressed a finger to his lips and slid his leather jacket fully open to expose the carabinieri shield he had clipped to the front of his blue jeans.

He stepped closer to the old woman. She was wearing a thin brown coat, a floppy hat, and thick-soled brown shoes. Murino pointed to the floor above. "Have you heard or seen anyone go upstairs?" he whispered.

The old woman nodded. "Three men," she said, answering in as low a voice as she could muster. "The middle apartment. They came in two days ago."

"Anyone else on this floor?" Murino asked. "Or the one above it?"

"Sometimes," she said. "But I haven't seen or heard anyone come or go. Except for the three I just mentioned."

"What's your name?"

"Carmela," the old woman said.

"Thank you, Carmela," Murino said. "Now, I need you to do me a favor."

"What?"

"Go back into your apartment," Murino said. "Lock the door

behind you. Go into your bedroom and don't come out, no matter what you hear. You stay there until I come back for you and tell you it's safe."

"Be careful," Carmela said. "Those men upstairs don't scare easy."

Murino smiled at Carmela. "Neither do I," he said.

10.

MURINO STOOD IN front of the door of the center apartment on the second floor. He listened to the sounds of utensils scraping against plates and glasses slamming against hard wood. He heard muffled voices and low laughter and a TV tuned to a soccer match. He made out three voices, all male; the loudest one was deep and guttural. Murino knew instantly it belonged to Guido Ostino, the most dangerous criminal in Florence, boss of the eighty-member-strong outfit known throughout the city and outlying regions as La Squadra Rossa (the Red Squad).

Guido Ostino was a child of the streets. He began his criminal career barely out of his teenage years, working as a drug runner for a local mob boss. He was smart and fearless and watched and learned how the boss ran his operation. In time, he recruited like-minded young men to his side with an eye on taking over the local boss's business. The local boss, sensing that the ambitious young man would soon be a threat to him, turned a potential enemy into a friend. He made him a full partner. Soon enough, Ostino was running the entire operation, throwing a percentage of the profits to his now elderly mentor.

But owning a piece of the criminal activity in Florence wasn't enough for a man like Guido Ostino. He wanted the whole city under his control. He recruited the youngest and most vicious street thugs into his crew and together they cut a bloody path through what had been a peaceful city.

There wasn't any crime that Ostino's crew would not commit so long as there was a profit to be had. He and his crew were hired out as assassins, paid to eliminate targets selected by crime bosses from the three organized factions spread throughout Italy. They killed at will, shook down shops big and small, controlled the drug and gambling operations in the city. They hijacked trucks, took over restaurants, charged high interest rates to those desperate for a euro bailout, and even took control of two local banks, using them to turn dirty money into clean.

On other occasions, it was more than rumored, they also did blood work for a handful of corrupt politicians and judges. Those jobs afforded Ostino an extra layer of protection, allowing him to go about his other illicit activities, feeling immune to any law enforcement interference.

That may have been true on the local level, with the municipal and local police departments on their trail, most lacking the funds and the manpower to go up against an organized crew like the one under Ostino's control. But it did not apply to Murino or any member of the carabinieri, the federal branch of Italian law enforcement. They had yet to be slandered by bribery or other forms of corruption and were respected by the law-abiding and feared by most of the criminal establishment. In many respects, the carabinieri, the equivalent of the FBI, are seen as the Untouchables of Italy.

The carabinieri have been, through the decades, the only arm of Italian law enforcement feared by any of the major organized crime gangs. They have been the ones to hunt down the mob bosses living in hiding, some for many years, and bring them to justice. They have chased down and captured gangs that have targeted judges for assassination, saved prosecutors from kidnappings, and protected those brave enough to testify in open court against a gangster on trial. On the streets of any city in Italy, the carabinieri are a welcome sight to those who live honest lives, while the underworld hides in the shadows whenever they get close.

Murino's hunger to nab Ostino went beyond professional reasons. His motives were personal. Three years earlier, Murino had befriended a troubled young woman, Claudia Morelli, as she was attempting to put a shattered life back together and provide for herself and her parents, both elderly and in need of care. To do so, she needed to shake free from the shackles of Guido Ostino. And, as anyone working the dark side of the streets of Florence could attest, that was no easy feat.

In desperate straits, Claudia had accepted a job offer from Ostino, happy to be hired as a hostess at one of the three restaurants he owned in the city. As it turned out, her responsibilities as a hostess required her to do more than welcome customers to the restaurant and show them to their seats. Long after closing time, she would be handed a heavy brown satchel, its contents never revealed. She was told to take the satchel to Piazzale Michelangelo and wait until a car stopped in front of her, headlights off. The rear window would be down. Inside would be a sealed white envelope. She was to place the heavy brown satchel in the back seat of the car and take out the envelope. No words or glances were to be exchanged between her and the driver.

She was then to go home and keep the envelope on her kitchen table and, in the morning, head out for a coffee, leaving the front door unlocked. When she returned, the envelope would be gone, replaced by a fifty-euro bill. No questions were to be asked, she was simply to do as she was told.

Claudia was grateful for the extra money, which helped, along with her hostess salary, to pay for backed-up bills and resident care for her parents.

All went smoothly for three months. Then, one morning, returning from her coffee run, instead of a fifty-euro bill resting on the center of her dining table, she found three detectives sitting around it.

Paolo Murino was one of them.

The young woman told the three detectives her story. Only one, Murino, believed her. It turned out the satchel was filled with large quantities of cocaine and the sealed white envelope contained the thousands of euros it cost to purchase the drug. Claudia was charged with possession and sale of a controlled substance and initially sentenced to a ten-year prison term. Murino interceded on her behalf and appealed to both the prosecutor in charge of the case and the judge presiding over it. He eventually convinced them that she was nothing more than a pawn who was told where to go and what to do. In return, she was paid a small pittance compared to what the dealers were taking in. "She's not your target," Murino said. "Ostino is the one we want and Ostino is the one we must get."

Claudia was released after serving two years in prison. She agreed to testify in open court to what she had been asked to do after each shift. Murino helped her land a job under an assumed name and find an affordable place to live. He asked the municipal police to keep an eye on her apartment building and be alert to any suspicious activity.

Murino would check in as often as he could, and through those weekly visits, a friendship blossomed. In that time, he would go with her to visit her parents, always aware that her life was in danger. He enjoyed his time in her company, smitten by a young woman with blue eyes that always seemed to sparkle and a smile that warmed his heart. He was very much aware that he could never get romantically involved with Claudia, knowing that that would cross a line not meant for a carabiniere to cross. She was under his protection and her life was in danger. Murino was determined that he would do all he could to ensure that nothing would happen to the young woman who had now become very much a part of his life.

And despite all the precautions that were put in place, Murino knew that so long as Ostino was a free man, her life would never be free from danger.

There was only one way to keep her safe.

Ostino needed to be taken down.

11.

MURINO SLID THE sharp edge of his switchblade into the lock chamber and moved it several times from left to right. After several seconds he heard the lock release. He pushed it open and entered the apartment. The three men, sitting at a small dining table, the remains of a pasta and grilled chicken dinner scattered around them, looked up when they saw him come in. Ostino, sitting directly across from where Murino stood, smiled.

"There's plenty more pasta in the kitchen," Ostino said. "Pull up a chair and we'll get you a plate."

Murino walked deeper into the room, holding his gun against his right leg. He shook his head. "I like to eat *after* I make an arrest," he said. "Never before."

"If it's me you came to arrest, I'm afraid you'll have to go without any dinner," Ostino said.

He eased back into his chair and grabbed an unlit cigar resting against a glass filled with red wine. His razor-cut white hair and trimmed beard stood in contrast to his all-black ensemble—blazer, polo shirt, slacks, and shoes. He was in his mid-fifties, short in stature but muscular in build. He stared at Murino for several moments and then shook his head. "You should know better than to come at me without backup," he said. "What do you expect to accomplish alone? Against the two I have sitting here with me? Not to mention the dozens hidden throughout this apartment building. Or did you fall for the act the sweet little old woman one floor down put on for you? She's my aunt, by the way. And she despises the police. The carabinieri most of all."

Murino shrugged. "I didn't want any backup," he said. "And while the old woman put on a good act, she wasn't very convincing. But, out of respect for my elders, I played along. Just so we're clear, I didn't come here for any of your men. That's a job I'll leave to the officers who have this building walled off and surrounded. As for me, well, I came here for you."

"Is there a specific charge you have in mind?" Ostino asked.

"Where to start?" Murino said. As he spoke, he edged closer to Ostino's side of the table. "I know about the drug dealing, so we'll kick it off with that one. That alone will be enough to put you away for a few decades. Then there's the judge and his family who died near the Ponte Vecchio."

"I read about that," Ostino said. "But if you're thinking I had anything to do with that tragedy, you should think again, carabiniere."

"I don't just think you had anything to do with that bombing," Murino said. "I know you did. You gave the order downstairs, sitting at your aunt's kitchen table. Lucky for us, we have the whole apartment wired. I know you think of her apartment as your safe zone. It isn't."

"Maybe I was just blowing off steam," Ostino said. He pushed back his chair and stood facing Murino. "Nothing more than that."

"Maybe," Murino said. "But you did more than blow off

steam when you shot and killed Franco Funelli. You remember him, don't you? A longtime member of your crew. He made the mistake, a fatal one as it turned out, of skimming some of the street money he oversaw collecting for you. You had to make an example of him. I understand how that goes. A magistrate might feel different. Especially when he gets a look at the CCTV footage that's been collected."

"You're forgetting someone," Ostino said. "That beautiful young girl you've got stashed away in what you and your friends think of as a safe house. She trusts you to protect her. That might be a mistake. A fatal one."

Murino raised his gun and pointed it at Ostino. "Walk toward me," he said. "And do it slowly, very slowly."

"A nod from me is all it will take for my two men to empty their guns into you," Ostino said.

"I know," Murino said. "But my gun isn't aimed at them. It's aimed at you. So, think before you nod."

Ostino stayed silent for a moment. He drew in a deep breath and walked slowly toward Murino, his arms spread away from his body.

"I don't think even you would shoot an unarmed man," he said to Murino.

"Depends on the man," Murino said.

Ostino stared at Murino for a moment and then rushed toward the carabiniere, catching him at chest level, both falling against the chipped marble floor. Murino's gun slipped from his hand, and he deflected two hard blows with his left arm. He saw the two men in the room still standing at the table, each with a gun in hand. Murino lifted his right hand and jammed a fist into

Ostino's Adam's apple, causing him to gag and ease his hold on him. He shoved Ostino off him, grabbed his gun, and fired off three rounds at the two men at the table. One bullet caught the first man in the shoulder, forcing him to drop his gun. A second shot creased one side of the other gunman's face. He screamed in pain and then lifted his gun and pointed it down at Murino.

Murino grabbed Ostino and brought him against his body, using him as a shield, forcing the gunman to hold his fire.

"Your finger touches that trigger, and he dies," Murino said.

Behind them, four armed carabinieri entered the apartment, weapons focused on the two wounded men.

Ostino held his place and smiled. "Let's both live to fight another day," he said.

"I look forward to it," Murino said.

Murino stood and lifted Ostino to his feet and wrapped a hand around his thick black belt. Together they moved out of the room. Once they were in the hall, heading toward the stairwell, Murino turned Ostino to face forward, and they began their descent.

Standing on each side of the steps and in front of each doorway were heavily armed carabinieri, in flak jackets and helmets, weapons at the ready. "I didn't want any backup," Murino whispered to Ostino, "but my boss insisted."

"You play me for a fool, Murino," he said. "That's a big mistake. One I'll make sure you pay for one day."

"I hope you enjoyed that pasta and chicken," Murino said. "It's the last good meal you're going to have for about four decades."

Murino turned the corner of the stairwell and handed Ostino

to two waiting carabinieri officers. They each grabbed one of his arms and dragged him down the final flight of stairs, out of the building, and into a waiting police van.

Murino spotted Carmela standing in front of her door, glaring at him. "You can rest easy now, Signora," he said to her, smiling. "These bad men will never bother you again. But you will get to see your nephew again. He's allowed one visitor a month."

"Laugh now," Carmela said. "Your time will come. My nephew will make you regret what you've done."

"Everyone's time comes sooner or later, Signora," Murino said.

He holstered his gun, gazed at the old woman, and then walked slowly out of the building and back out into the courtyard.

12.

"OSTINO WAS ARRESTED and eventually sentenced to thirty years in prison," Captain Murino said, walking down the sloping hill toward Nonna Maria's house. Her left arm rested comfortably in the crook of his folded right elbow. "Then we went after the members of the Red Squad."

Nonna Maria glanced at the captain. She noticed a slight change to the tenor of his voice, his body tense, his normally confident manner giving off a semblance of regret. "We hunted them down, each and every one," he said. "And we didn't stop until they were all captured or killed. It was a brutal time. There was so much violence, so much bloodshed, so many lives lost, on both sides."

"And those dark days and nights were what led you to request a transfer to Ischia," Nonna Maria said.

"Yes," the captain said, glancing at Nonna Maria. "But how do you know I requested a transfer? How do you know I wasn't simply assigned here?"

"The carabinieri normally sent to Ischia are new to the job or one step away from retirement," Nonna Maria said. "Not highly decorated young officers like you. At least that's what the talk was among those who like to talk when you first arrived."

"I always wanted to be a member of the carabinieri," the captain said. "Ever since I can remember. But that one year spent chasing the members of the Red Squad made me question my dedication and devotion to the job. I had turned into something I no longer recognized. I became obsessed with their capture, the hunt, the chase, all of it. And I found myself at ease with the violence. When it was over, I took some time off, rented a cabin in Umbria, and spent my days thinking about what kind of a future I wanted. My nights were spent reliving the nightmare I had left behind in Florence."

"You saved many lives doing what you did," Nonna Maria said. "That should have helped you live with what you had to do."

"To a degree," Captain Murino said. "But, in many ways, I'm still haunted by those days. Florence is the city of Michelangelo and Dante. And I helped turn it into a shooting gallery, each night a body found on one of those historic streets, a white sheet covering another member taken down. It made me realize I was never meant to be the great carabinieri officer I had hoped to become."

Nonna Maria smiled at the captain. "It also made you realize something else," she said. "Something more important than being a great carabinieri officer."

"What?"

"That you're a good man," Nonna Maria said.

Captain Murino clasped one of her hands in his and gently gave it a squeeze. "If I am, it's from spending the past six years here, on this island, in the company of the ones fortunate enough to make Ischia their home. And with a friend like you always there to lend a helping hand."

Nonna Maria stopped at the base of the steps leading to her two-story house. She rested a hand on top of the black iron railing. "The ones who might be here and the ones still to come that mean you harm, what is their connection to the man you arrested in Florence?"

"Ostino still has a great deal of power in his end of the criminal world," Captain Murino said. "Being behind bars doesn't lessen that for a man like him. If there are people coming to the island looking to bring me harm, they would be here on his orders and his money."

"One of them might already be here, Captain," Nonna Maria said. "Il Presidente met with a man earlier today. He is pretty sure he was sent here by someone from the North. And, from what he's told me, he believes more are on the way."

13.

THE FOUR MEN sat at a rear table in the dimly lit mountain restaurant. A bottle of red wine and one of sparkling mineral water rested in the center of the table. The water glasses were empty, the wine glasses full. A young waiter approached the table. "Sorry to interrupt," he said in a low voice. "Do you need a moment, or would you like to hear our specials for today?"

"No need," the oldest of the four men said. "We know what we want. First, two more bottles of wine, and keep bringing them until I signal you to stop."

"Not a problem," the waiter said.

"Assorted antipasti for the table," the older man said. "Pasta with clams and broccoli rabe, easy on the garlic, heavy on the red pepper flakes. And two brick-oven-cooked rabbits in a tomato and herb sauce with a green salad on the side dressed in oil and lemon. And espresso with Sambuca and coffee beans for after. Lots of espresso. Hope I made that easy for you."

"The easiest and best order I'll get all night," the waiter said, smiling and walking from the table.

The men waited until the waiter disappeared around a corner, and then the more agitated of the group turned to his right to face the oldest, Maurizio Carnale. "So, other than dinner, why did you risk exposing the job by sending for the three of us?" he asked.

"The job is already exposed, Marco," Carnale said.

"How so?" Marco said, tossing a quick glance at the two men sitting on either side.

"I got a surprise visit today from somebody I had written off as dead," Carnale said. "A guy that years ago, each of us would have taken a step back if we had to come up against him."

"You going to tell us who it was or you going to make us guess?" Marco asked, not bothering to mask any sign of his annoyance.

"Il Presidente," Carnale said. "Came up and sat across from me while I was having a coffee down at the port."

"Who is that?" the young man to Marco's right asked.

"Before your time, Luigi," Carnale said, shrugging his massive shoulders. He turned to his left. "And yours too, Aldo. Just so you don't ask me the same question he just did."

Marco took a sip of wine and stayed silent for a few moments. While the two younger men were dressed in casual outfits of tight white T-shirts and jeans, Marco came to dinner in more stylish attire. He was wearing a long-sleeved black button-down shirt, tailored gray slacks, and brown Ferragamo loafers. "From what I've heard, he was in the business for many years," he finally said. "And he's been out of it even longer. He might have done some work with one of the crews up north. That's not out of the question. Might have kept in touch with one or two of them."

"All that may be true, Marco," Carnale said. "But none of that explains how he knew I would be in Ischia or what I'm doing here."

"Will one of you tell me who this guy is?" Aldo said. "First of all, why is he called Il Presidente?"

"How he got the name, I don't know," Carnale said. "My guess is he was so good at what he did, someone gave him that as a nickname. As far as I can tell, nobody knows his real name."

"How good was he?" Luigi asked.

Marco waited for the waiter to place two large platters in the center of the table, one filled with warm antipasti and the other with cold.

"I'll be back in a minute with more bread and wine," he said.

"How good was Il Presidente?" Carnale said once the waiter had left. "In his time, alone he was better than the four of us combined."

"And now?" Aldo asked.

"I don't know," Marco said, turning his gaze to Carnale. "You sat across from him. How did he look to you?"

"A lot older than I imagined he would," Carnale said. "But he was in good shape, a little slower maybe, but not somebody you would be quick to ignore. The fact he's even here could be a problem."

"We crossed paths years ago," Marco said. "I didn't work with him. Nobody really did. He was a loner; my guess is he still is. But the job he went out on that I knew about was handled quietly and quickly. He showed no mercy. Not back then."

"It seemed odd to me a guy like Il Presidente would connect to a carabinieri captain," Carnale said. "After he left, I asked around about him. Have a couple of cousins that live on the island. I went to see them to see if they could help me out."

"Did they?" Aldo asked.

Carnale speared a forkful of roasted peppers and dried sausage and nodded. "He lives with an old widow woman," he said. "They call her Nonna Maria, and she has helped the captain with a couple of his cases the past few summers."

"Helped how?" Marco asked.

"They weren't too clear on that," Carnale said. "But if Il Presidente connects to the carabinieri captain, it's through this Nonna Maria. It's the only explanation that fits."

The waiter arrived with a fresh basket of bread and a newly opened bottle of Brunello. Marco took the wine from the waiter and waved him away. "I'll take it from here," he said. "You go check on the rabbit."

Marco filled the wine glasses around the table and then rested the bottle next to his elbow. "I'll go back in the morning and report on what I heard here tonight," he said. "Luigi and Aldo will stay behind and work with you until I return. For now, let's keep our focus on the job. The sooner that happens, the sooner we can all clear out."

"And if Il Presidente and the widow lady get in the way?" Carnale asked.

"Il Presidente is looking to protect this Nonna Maria," Marco said. "That's who he cares about. Is that your impression, too?"

Carnale nodded. "She seemed to be his concern," he said. "His only concern, from what I could tell."

"The easy answer is that when we make a move on the captain, we do it when he's not around the widow," Marco said. "We do that, we won't give Il Presidente cause to step into the fight."

"What if we can't get to him without the widow woman in the way?" Carnale asked.

Marco shrugged. "Then we get her out of the way," he said.

"Same goes for Il Presidente. We can't let either one keep us from doing what we're here to do."

"I'll do what I signed on to do," Carnale said. "We're here to be either shooters or decoys. Either way works for me. But there's going to be blowback enough from being any part of taking down a carabinieri captain. Toss a dead widow into the mix, and that could bring even more heat our way."

"We do what is asked of us," Marco said. "That's why we were hired."

"I haven't said a word since I got the call two weeks ago," Carnale said. "And yet, my first day on the island, drinking my first cup of coffee of the morning, I get a visit from none other than Il Presidente."

"And that tells you what?" Marco asked, leaning closer to the table.

"Somebody on our side talked," Carnale said. "And if that talk made its way to Il Presidente, it might have reached not only the widow woman but the carabinieri captain as well."

Marco glared at Carnale. "You really know how to kill a man's appetite," he said.

He pushed his chair back and stood. He reached into a front pocket of his jeans and pulled out a thick roll of euros. He peeled off five fifty-euro bills and tossed them on the center of the table. "Enjoy the rabbit," he said. "My treat."

Marco turned and made his way out of the crowded restaurant.

Sitting in a dark corner of the bar near the entrance, a black Borsalino hat resting low on his head, Il Presidente ignored Marco and kept his eyes on the three remaining men at the table.

An elderly bartender with a thin blue sweater draped over his shoulders walked over to Il Presidente and nodded at his empty glass. "Can I get you anything else?" he asked.

Il Presidente nodded. "A phone," he said. "Not the one next to the liquor bottles. The burner you keep in the register."

14.

NONNA MARIA POURED her fourth cup of espresso of the morning. Her nephew and doctor, Agostino, leaned against the dining room table and shook his head. "It's bad enough you drink about fourteen cups of coffee each day," he said. "But you could at least try to hide it while I'm here. As a favor to your doctor, if for no other reason."

"You're not just my doctor, Agostino," Nonna Maria said. "You're my nephew. And I keep nothing from you. There are no secrets between us."

"Do you still put three small pieces of chocolate in each cup?" Agostino asked. "Along with three sugars and a touch of Stock 84?"

Nonna Maria shrugged. "It's the way I like it," she said. "And they tell me it's good for the heart."

"Who tells you?" Agostino asked, not bothering to hide his smile.

"People talk about many things, Agostino," Nonna Maria said. "Most of the talk doesn't interest me. But if it's about coffee or wine, I listen."

"Don't get me started on the wine," Agostino said. "It is hard for me to believe that a woman your age, who drinks only coffee during the day and wine at night and helps chase down criminals the rest of the time, is in such good physical condition. I'm more than happy about it. I simply don't understand how it's possible."

"It could be because I never drink water," Nonna Maria said. "Perhaps you should pass that on to your other patients. And I don't spend my time chasing down criminals. I help my friends. Nothing more to it than that."

"Speaking of your friends," Agostino said, "I understand there could be trouble brewing for the carabinieri captain. Any truth to it?"

"Where did you hear that?" Nonna Maria asked.

"You're not the only one who hears people talk, Zia," Agostino said. "I see dozens of patients a week, either in my studio or at their homes. They all have something to say. Most of the time, I don't pay much attention to the talk. It's nothing more than idle gossip. But sometimes I do listen."

"Sit and have a coffee with me," Nonna Maria said. "If fourteen cups a day can't do me any harm, one cup should not cause you any problems."

Agostino nodded. He pulled out a hard-backed chair and sat down across from Nonna Maria. She reached for an empty cup and lifted a large espresso pot to fill it. "I'm guessing you would prefer to have it without the chocolate, sugar, and Stock 84," she said.

"Good guess, Zia," Agostino said.

"When you were finishing your medical studies, you were offered many jobs from different hospitals in the North," Nonna Maria said. "I remember your mother was so excited, she could barely keep track of all of them."

"Five hospitals offered me full-time positions," Agostino said. "I did my residency at the main hospital in Florence and then came back here and began my practice."

"I remember how much you enjoyed your time in Florence," Nonna Maria said.

"Very much," Agostino said. "Even though there isn't much in the way of free time during a medical residency. But Florence is, in so many ways, a magical city. There is history on practically any street you walk. In my free time, I toured Michelangelo's home and walked through the room where Dante wrote *The Inferno*. And I had two favorite places I would visit any chance I could—Santa Croce and the pharmacy."

Nonna Maria smiled. She loved Agostino as much as if he were one of her own sons, and it was a point of pride to her that he chose to practice medicine in Ischia, caring for the people of the island, instead of taking one of the more lucrative offers that were available to him at one of the hospitals in the North. She worried about him as much as he worried about her. Nonna Maria felt he neglected his own health in caring for the sick and infirm of Ischia.

Agostino was in his mid-fifties, slender, with razor-cut sandy gray hair and a relaxed and affable manner. He always wore a crisp white shirt, the sleeves rolled to the elbows, slacks, and comfortable walking shoes. He worked long hours, making house calls from early in the morning until long after the sun went down. He doted on his patients and, on days he worked out of his studio, on the far end of Via Roma, his waiting room was always filled.

He was a devoted family man, happily married for many decades to Pina Longo, whom he met on the Maronti beach when both were still in their teens. His wife, in addition to helping raise their three children, also handled the bookkeeping end of his medical practice. In his free moments, he would often lose himself in the pages of a book—thrillers and historical novels were among his favorites.

"I have heard about Santa Croce," Nonna Maria said. "It's a church. My granddaughter Alessandra told me about it. She lives in an apartment close to it. She's there, as you know, studying to be a lawyer."

"It's more than just a church, Zia," Agostino said. "It's where the greats of the Renaissance are buried, from Michelangelo to Galileo to Machiavelli. I would spend entire afternoons just staring up at all the tombs. Standing there in the shadow of giants. You should see it. You would be amazed."

Nonna Maria nodded. "I am seeing it," she said. "Through your eyes. You have painted a beautiful picture for me."

"And the pharmacy is not too far away from the church," Agostino said. "And, in its own way, is just as special a place. It's been around since the thirteenth century and once sold herbs and medicinal powders to some of the very men buried inside Santa Croce. They would take them to cure themselves of a variety of ailments, from arthritis to gout to constipation."

"It's a city that honors its dead and respects its past," Nonna Maria said. "But it must also have seen its share of troubles. Back then as well as up to today. Even a beautiful city must have an ugly side they like to keep hidden from view."

"They have their share of crime, as all large and small cities do," Agostino said. "I believe Captain Murino would know that side of Florence better than I would. But to be fair, I always felt safe in the years I lived and studied there."

"This talk you heard about Captain Murino among your patients," Nonna Maria said. "Did it sound to you like more than gossip?"

"I'm afraid it did," Agostino said. "Many of my patients have friends and relatives living in the North. Murino, it seems, made a name for himself in Florence, and attracted some attention during his years there, primarily from his street battles with a gang known as the Red Squad. It was a large and brutal gang that earned great profits but brought only misery and pain to those innocents who crossed their path. Murino led the carabinieri team that brought them to justice."

"I was told the leader of this gang is in prison," Nonna Maria said. "Held there for many years."

Agostino stood up, put on his jacket, and reached for his black medical bag. "Zia, there are some men who are as much of a danger inside a prison as they were when they were free," he said. "The one Murino helped put away is such a man. I know there's nothing I can say that will keep you from doing all you can to help the captain. Especially if you believe his life to be at risk. All I ask is that you be careful. And if I can help in any way, know that you can both count on me."

Nonna Maria embraced Agostino and walked him toward her front door. "I thought I was the one in the family who helped her friends," she said, giving him a warm smile.

Agostino kissed her on both cheeks and embraced his favorite aunt. "Don't let it get around," he whispered in her ear. "My days and nights are busy enough as it is."

"Not to worry," Nonna Maria said. "I'm as good at keeping secrets as I am at helping my friends."

15.

NONNA MARIA SAT on a stone bench, the massive shadow of the Castello Aragonese looming over her left shoulder. Behind her, the Pirate hauled his motorboat onto the sands of a small beach, then turned and walked toward her, waving as he did. He was a short, wiry man, with skin the color of old leather sandals. He had a white beard, long sandy hair secured by two thick bands, and a red bandanna wrapped around his head. He was wearing a cream-colored short-sleeved shirt, unbuttoned, the front flaps knotted at his waist, and a red Speedo. He wore no shoes and approached her with a wide smile on his heavily lined face.

He stopped several feet from Nonna Maria and pointed in the direction of a café across from where she was sitting. "I've been under the hot sun all day," he said. "I need a cold drink. I'll get two in case you want to join me."

Nonna Maria shook her head. "I only drink what comes out of my kitchen," she said. "You know me well enough to know that."

"Indeed I do," the Pirate said. "I just needed an excuse to order two cold beers. Makes me look like the gentleman I'm not, instead of the drunk I am."

Nonna Maria waited as the Pirate went into the cool interior of the café and came out carrying two bottles of Peroni, paid for with the loose change he kept in his shirt pocket. He walked over and sat next to her on the stone bench. He rested one bottle of beer on the short wall above them and took a long drink from the other. "It's good to see you again, Nonna Maria," the Pirate said. "It's been too long. When you get to be our age, you shouldn't let too much time pass between visits."

"I'm glad my cousin Gigi found you," Nonna Maria said, "and told you I needed to talk to you."

The Pirate took another swallow of beer and nodded. "He woke me from my nap," he said. "Took his boat out to where I was anchored and tossed a bucket of water over my side. Told me to make it down here by nightfall and come see you."

Nonna Maria lifted her large black tote bag from between her feet and rested it on the stone seat between herself and the Pirate. "I need your help," she said. "But before we get to that, I brought you something to go with those beers."

"I knew you'd have a feast prepared," the Pirate said. "If the Good Lord Jesus had had you with him on the beach that day, those five thousand people would have eaten a lot more than some bread and a few fish, that's for certain."

"I brought you enough to eat tonight and for tomorrow while you're out at sea," Nonna Maria said.

She eased two large plastic shopping bags from her tote bag and handed them to the Pirate.

"I made you a roast chicken," she said. "I cooked it Ischia style, drenched in white wine and herbs, wrapped in thick foil and buried under the sand, left to cook under the hot sun for four hours. There's also marinated mushrooms, stuffed peppers, pasta with sausage and broccoli rabe, steak pizzaiola, fresh-baked bread, a container of olive oil, and two bottles of D'Ambra wine, one red, one white."

"You're a gift from the gods, Nonna Maria," the Pirate said. "I haven't eaten all day and don't remember eating anything yesterday either. Would you think me rude if I ate while we talked?"

Nonna Maria smiled. "There are knives and forks in each bag," she said. "And enough napkins to keep your shirt and beard clean."

The Pirate peered into the bags and reached for a large bowl double-wrapped in cellophane. He pulled it out of the bag, removed the cellophane, and smiled. "Just the smell alone is enough to satisfy any man," he said, staring down at the still-warm double serving of penne with broccoli rabe and sausage.

"There's a small bowl of cheese in there and a hot red pepper," Nonna Maria said. "In case you want to give it some extra flavor."

The Pirate jammed a forkful of the pasta into his mouth and nodded. "I've been lucky enough in life to have enjoyed many wonderful meals," he said. "But I've yet to taste anything as delicious as what comes out of your kitchen. You missed your calling, Nonna Maria. You could have been as famous as that chef whose name everyone knows and whose recipes they are all anxious to follow."

"I just buy the food," Nonna Maria said. "My stove does all the work."

The Pirate grabbed a folded napkin and wiped his lips and then looked at Nonna Maria. "I'm going to save the rest of the beer for later. And drink some of the wine you were kind enough to bring along with the food," he said. "And nothing goes better with a good bottle of D'Ambra wine than a talk between two old friends."

"Years ago, you ran cigarette boats between the island and Naples," Nonna Maria said. "Running contraband items in return for cash. There was a lot of money to be made during the seventies and eighties on those boats. The kind that needed to be hidden from view."

The Pirate smiled and nodded. "It was almost impossible to get caught," he said. "The carabinieri back then didn't have boats that could catch a cigarette boat. We were much too fast for them. And most of the time we moved at night. They could hear our motors and maybe catch a glimpse of the boat, especially if there was a full moon. But the only way either the carabinieri or the Coast Guard could ever grab one of us was if the boat broke down."

"There were a number of people who did well during those years," Nonna Maria said. "They bought homes, started a business, retired young, all from the profits made running cigarettes, wine, and other contraband items."

"But not drugs," the Pirate said. "The law didn't really care about cigarettes or wine, or olive oil, being sold free of government stamps or approval. But the ones who moved drugs, they did all right for a while. Some even better than all right. But sooner or later, they were the ones who were caught, arrested, and sent away for many years."

"Tell me about the caves around the island," Nonna Maria said. "How did you make use of them?"

"The caves offered us safety," the Pirate said. "A place to hide our boats, our money, our goods. If you knew how to make use of the caves, then you were more than just one step ahead of the authorities. You were kilometers ahead of anyone looking to either catch you or steal your goods."

"Since I was a young girl, I've heard many stories about the tunnels inside the caves," Nonna Maria said. "How they were used centuries ago by the Greeks and then the Romans, either to hide from the ships of approaching enemies or to store goods and weapons."

"Those tunnels were also used by both the Allies and the Nazis back when they occupied the island during World War II," the Pirate said. "Often for the same reasons as the Greeks and Romans. And back even further by the Moors during the two hundred or so years they had control of Ischia."

"You've been inside those tunnels?" Nonna Maria asked.

"Many times," the Pirate said. "There are so many of them that they were even given names, to distinguish one from the other. They are very easy to get into, but unless you know exactly which way to go, they can be impossible to get out of. Quite a few men have died over the years, unable to find an exit from the tunnels."

"What makes it so hard?"

"There's one tunnel, over in Barano, by the rocks shaped like an elephant's tusks, and it has a number of openings that if you're not careful will seal up after you pass through," the Pirate said. "Now, that could just be a tall tale told to frighten away those on the hunt. Or it could be true. I was never curious enough to find out for myself."

"What if you were given a reason to be curious," Nonna Maria said. "Would you go back into those caves again?"

"I was nervous enough going in as a young man," the Pirate said. "And I went only into the tunnels where I knew how to navigate the path out. I'm a lot older now, so I would need a good reason to convince me to overlook the dangers of going back in. And, sitting here now, next to you, I can't begin to think of one."

"Would a search for a lost treasure be a good enough reason?" Nonna Maria asked.

The Pirate stared at Nonna Maria for a moment, took a long swig from the bottle of white wine, and smiled. "I would be a sorry excuse for a pirate if I weren't interested in a search for lost treasure," he said. "But I practically lived in those tunnels during the contraband years, and I've read as much as I could about them. But I never saw or heard any mention of a lost treasure hidden in those tunnels. And if I hadn't, how did you?"

"A friend mentioned it," Nonna Maria said. "It was a story passed on to her by her grandfather, on his deathbed. He didn't live long enough to tell her the full story or even what the lost treasure was. All she knows is that whatever this treasure is, it is hidden in the caves."

"That's all she has?" the Pirate asked. "The words of a man soon to die?"

"She also has a map," Nonna Maria said.

"And you agreed to help her find it?" the Pirate asked.

Nonna Maria smiled. "I was hoping it would be with the help of a friend," she said.

The Pirate leaned against the cold stone wall and closed his eyes for several moments. He stayed still as he spoke. "This treasure could be anything," he said. "If it even exists. Could be a family heirloom. Some trinkets that will mean nothing to anyone but this woman. Or it could be something of great value, hidden away for years. But once word gets out—and trust me, when it comes to something like this, word will get out, no matter how careful you are—they will come to Ischia in packs looking for the lost treasure."

"Who will come looking?" Nonna Maria asked.

"Treasure hunters, real pirates, mercenaries, thieves," the Pirate said. "Even the organized mobs in Naples and Sicily might get curious enough to send a few of their men. Even a hint of a possible discovery is enough to lure them out."

"But none of them know these waters and those tunnels as well as you," Nonna Maria said.

The Pirate nodded. "I do know the waters and the caves as well as anyone who might come looking," he said. "But as far as the tunnels go, you will need someone better than me. Someone who knows every hidden curve, which stone to move to seal a wall, and not only the best way into the tunnels, but the best way out."

"And is this someone you know?" Nonna Maria asked.

"Yes," the Pirate said. "We worked together for several years a long time ago. If you're going after anything lost in those caves, treasure or otherwise, he's the one we need."

"Do you trust him?"

The Pirate shook his head. "In that end of the business, it's best not to trust anyone. But in all our years together, he always held to his end of the deal. And that's as much as you can ask."

"Will he help us?" Nonna Maria asked.

"Yes," the Pirate said. "But he never did anything for free, and I can't see him finding religion now."

"How long before we can get him to Ischia?"

"Won't take long at all," the Pirate said. "He lives here on the island. Has a beachfront house just outside of Forio. If I had saved my money the way he did, I'd be living the same way."

"What's his name?" Nonna Maria asked.

"That will be harder to find than any lost treasure," the Pirate said. He stood, finished off the last of the wine, and picked up his bags of food and drink. "He goes by the name he's been called since he first started running contraband from Naples to the island so many years ago. A name even you, Nonna Maria, have probably heard."

"What name?"

"The Magician," the Pirate said.

16.

IL PRESIDENTE WALKED down the dark and sloping road from the Monte Corvo restaurant, the shimmering glow from the houses and boats of the harbor below and the sparkle from the stars in the sky above offering the only light for his path. He walked with one hand in his pants pocket and the other holding a lit cigarette, his head down, lost in a whirlwind of thoughts. He had never laid eyes on those four men in the restaurant above until this day, but he knew them as if they had been raised in the same family.

There was a time when he had done what they now did, allowing men to pay him to bring harm to others.

Il Presidente was an only child, his father unknown to him and his mother cast aside from both her family and her friends, alone and shunned. She died at an early age, leaving Il Presidente to scrounge for food and shelter, his days and nights filled with the tormented memories of the life his mother had been forced to live.

She had once been a woman filled with promise, eager to embark on a path that would allow her to fulfill her long-held dreams. Her happy journey was derailed by a missed train connection in Naples leading her to wander down the wrong streets in a city whose beauty, much like that of any other big city, can often disguise its dangers. It would take ten years for her to re-emerge and return to the island of Ischia, a young son grasping tightly onto her side.

Il Presidente's life had offered him few choices—he was alone, in some cases hated, in others feared. On an island filled with beauty and sunshine, he knew only ugliness and darkness. Such a life led him to make the only choice he felt he could make—he would enter a world of violence and menace and, if he was indeed to be hated and feared, give people a reason to fear him.

Il Presidente became a criminal.

He thrived for decades, becoming a dangerous force whose very name was synonymous with death and violence. And while such a fearsome reputation earned him respect in the world of the criminal elite, it did not change his status among the people whose affection he most craved—the men and women of the island he called home.

And in these four men, faces new to the island but ones he so easily recognized from his years in the dark world, he saw danger.

He lit a fresh cigarette and stopped at a bend in the road, leaning against an iron railing, staring down at the lights below.

He had a gnawing feeling about those four men. Four men new to the island, not familiar with the target, not knowing his habits, his schedule, where he lived, where he ate, who he spent his off-hours with, would not be sent to do a job that needed to be done professionally and skillfully. Yes, they could ambush the carabinieri captain, take him down when he wasn't expecting it, but that came with a great deal of risk and exposure.

This job, to Il Presidente's way of thinking, would belong to one man, someone already living on the island. Someone who might even know the captain, someone the captain might even consider a friend. One man with experience and a personal reason to take out the captain. And it would probably be someone with a connection to the mob boss the carabinieri captain helped put away eight years ago. A relative or someone who had reason to want to avenge the crime boss.

Ostino had been in prison for eight years. If he wanted to send paid assassins to go after the carabinieri captain, he would have no reason to wait this long. Hired guns can be bought at any time, for any price.

No, this hit was personal. That meant the boss needed to wait until his chosen shooter was experienced enough to do the job and close enough to the captain not to arouse suspicion.

Il Presidente tossed his cigarette to the ground, stomped it out with the heel of his thick-soled shoe, and continued his slow walk down to the port and Nonna Maria's house.

He would deal with the four men sent here, most likely as decoys, perhaps eager to make a run at the carabinieri captain to prove their mettle to the one who sent them.

But the one he needed to find was a more elusive and dangerous foe.

An assassin hiding in plain sight.

17.

CAPTAIN MURINO WALKED up the steps of the Castello Aragonese, Nonna Maria by his side. The steps were steep and wide. A hard five-story climb for anyone, especially an elderly woman on a hot summer morning. "It would be easier, not to mention faster, if we took the elevator to the top," the captain said, glancing over at Nonna Maria.

"I've been walking to the top of this castle since I was a child," Nonna Maria said. "I don't see a reason why I should stop now. I may be slow, but I'm steady. And we can rest whenever we feel the need. The walk will do us both some good."

"I don't want you to get hurt," Captain Murino said. "I'm not talking about our climb to the top of the castle. These men that have come to bring me down, they will not hesitate to harm anyone that stands between them and me. I know how much you want to help. But this is one case you had best stay clear of. I need to go into this with a clear head, and I won't have that if I think you will be in any danger."

Nonna Maria stopped, leaned against a stone wall, and waited as she caught her breath. She pulled a thick white handkerchief from a pocket of her black dress and wiped her upper lip and forehead. "Have you made your men aware of the danger you face?" she asked.

Captain Murino shook his head. "This is my fight," he said, "not theirs. Many of them are newly graduated from the academy and have neither the skill nor the experience to go up against the men I'll need to confront. Their job will be to protect the locals and tourists from harm. The rest will be up to me."

"I know you're trying to protect me and are concerned about me," Nonna Maria said. "And for that you have my heart. But you will need me and the others who will be by my side to help you fight these men."

"Need you in what way, Nonna Maria?" the captain asked. "These men are stone cold killers. This isn't anything like the past cases you helped me on. This isn't a con woman looking to scam money from a hotel and blame your goddaughter for a theft that never happened. These men are good at only one thing—and that's ending someone's life. I've been up against them, and I know best how to stop them."

"They may know how to kill," Nonna Maria said, "but they don't know this island. Everywhere they go, they will have eyes on them. In a big city like Florence, they can hide. Not here on Ischia. I will know where they go, where they eat, where they sleep. They will never be out of sight. And that alone should be a big help to you."

Captain Murino looked at Nonna Maria and shook his head. "It's crazy for me to even think I could stop you from doing whatever you wanted to do," he said. "So, if I can't do that, would it do any good for me to at least ask you to be careful?"

Nonna Maria shrugged. "I'm always careful," she said, resuming her climb up the castle steps. "It's how you get to be old."

"How often do you make the climb to the top?" Captain Murino asked.

"Not as much as I once did," Nonna Maria said. "When my Gabriel was alive, we would come here on Sunday afternoons, especially during the summer months, sometimes alone, sometimes with the children. The air was always cooler at the top, and the views are the best you'll find on Ischia."

"This castle has seen many a battle down the centuries," Captain Murino said. "It has quite a history. I was most impressed with the medieval torture museum on the next floor. I went to see it my first week on the island. There are weapons there I had only read about in adventure novels. And some I had no idea even existed."

"The castle is Ischia's great protector," Nonna Maria said. "But, like many such places, it has its own dark history. Have you been to the Cemetery of Dead Nuns? It's one floor below the torture museum."

Captain Murino shook his head. "I didn't know there was a cemetery in the castle. How could I have missed it all the times I've visited?"

"It's not what we would consider a normal cemetery," Nonna Maria said. "It's the Cemetery of Dead Nuns, nuns from the Order of Saint Clare. They were living here at the castle centuries ago. When the nuns died, they were not buried. Their bodies were left on a stone seat, called the death chair, each one in a sitting position. The death seats are still there for us to see."

"What was the purpose of the death seat?"

"I only know what my mother told me when she first took me to see the cemetery," Nonna Maria said. "She pointed out the hole in the center of the death chair. It was there to collect the fluids from the body as the corpses began to rot. Once they were down to bones, the remains would be removed from the death chair and taken to a final resting place."

"A sad ending for anyone," Captain Murino said, "let alone a nun."

"Each day, the nuns of the order would visit the cemetery and pray," Nonna Maria said. "They would kneel before the decomposing bodies and reflect on their own mortality. Sometimes the nuns, young and old, would stay for hours, eyes closed, hands folded. But spending that much time, that close to rotting bodies, every day, came with a price."

"The nuns risked disease and death," Captain Murino said. "You cannot spend that much time in front of a decomposing body without being exposed to so many illnesses."

"Many of them did die horrible deaths," Nonna Maria said. "Deaths that did not have to happen. But it was the way of the order, and for those nuns it was the only life they knew. A death chair was there, waiting for each one. But still they went in, without any fear."

Captain Murino stayed silent for a moment and then turned to Nonna Maria. "I'm not sure I would have been able to do what those nuns did," he said. "I don't think I have that kind of courage."

"You have plenty of courage, Captain," Nonna Maria said. "You have faced down death many times yourself. You may not have prayed in a room filled with decaying nuns. Your courage came in a different form, but it was still there, and you never took a step back. Just like those nuns from long ago, you never showed fear."

"But the fear was always there, Nonna Maria," Captain Murino said. "It was there back in Florence. And it's here with me now. I will be going up against men who would like nothing better than to see my body rotting on one of those death chairs in the cemetery."

Nonna Maria placed her hand under Captain Murino's left arm, and they continued their slow walk to the top of the castle. "Never lose that fear, Captain," she said. "It's what helps keep us alive. In many ways, it is better to be afraid than to have courage."

Captain Murino glanced at Nonna Maria and smiled. "And what is it you fear, Nonna Maria?" he asked.

"A day without coffee and a night without wine," Nonna Maria said.

18.

NONNA MARIA ALWAYS looked forward to Sunday afternoons. That was when her family, along with several of her friends, would gather at her home and enjoy a long meal together. Nonna Maria loved preparing the feast, though she never ate with them, preferring to sit with a cup of coffee or a cold glass of wine and listen to the stories told and the laughter that often followed the tales. Especially the gleeful sounds made by her grandchildren and great-grandchildren. She always took her meals sitting at her dining room table on the chair facing the portrait of her late husband, Gabriel. The meal hours had been their time together when he was alive, and Nonna Maria saw no need to change their routine simply because he had died.

They met when both were teenagers and married when they were barely free of those awkward years. "My parents had a love affair that began on the first day they met and that lives to this day," Nunzia, Nonna Maria's youngest daughter, would often tell friends. "He was the only man for her, and she was the only woman for him. Everyone wonders why she prefers to eat her meals alone. But she's not alone. She sits across from his portrait, and in those moments, they are together, just the two of them. He is always at her side. In death as in life."

On this Sunday afternoon, Il Presidente stood in the entrance to the kitchen. Nonna Maria had her back to him, easing a large tray of eggplant and chicken parmigiana out of the oven. "The smells coming out of this kitchen have reached all the way to Via Roma," he said with a smile. "There are two large tables in the garden and one in the dining room. But, in case we find ourselves with some uninvited guests, I had Peppino bring down another table from his kitchen."

"All are welcome," Nonna Maria said. "My kitchen is closed to no one who brings with them an appetite and a warm heart. I hope you didn't eat too much of the antipasti. I made some of your favorites today. You're the guest of honor. You sit at the head of the table, the place where my Gabriel used to sit."

"You didn't need to go to any trouble," Il Presidente said, his thick voice cracking just a bit. "Especially not for me."

Nonna Maria wiped her hands on a dish towel and walked over to Il Presidente, leaned up and gave him a warm kiss on his cheek. "Happy birthday, my dear friend," she whispered.

"How did you know?" Il Presidente asked, not bothering to hide his surprise.

Nonna Maria shrugged. "I remembered an earlier one, back when you were a boy," she said. "I know you're a private man and don't want people to know, and they won't. This celebration today will be our secret. Just the two of us. But you deserve a day in your honor. And it brings a smile to my face to be able to give it to you."

Il Presidente's eyes were moist with tears, and for a few moments he stood there staring at this old woman who had rescued him from the darkness of a cold world and given him a reason to live and someone to love. "I don't know what to say, Nonna

Maria," he said, his voice barely above a whisper. "Or how to ever thank you."

"I know how you can thank me," Nonna Maria said. "You can start bringing the food out and help get this feast going. Even the birthday boy must work today."

Within minutes, the tables were filled with platters of grilled chicken with vinegar peppers; marinated branzino cooked in a wood oven, covered by a topping of lemon, capers, and white wine; grilled calamari nestled alongside roasted peppers, fresh mozzarella, and basil; linguini with clams and mussels in a fresh tomato sauce; tricolore pasta in a pesto sauce; fresh-baked bread toasted and covered with tiny sun-dried tomatoes and black olives. White and red wine flowed and sounds of laughter echoed past the corridor leading out of Nonna Maria's garden, reaching as far as the crowded local beach less than a quarter of a mile away.

Nonna Maria moved from table to table, enjoying the stories that were told and reveling in the pure joy of the family and friends in her company. "Mama, do you remember when Mario and Joseph would give Papa his weekly shave on Sunday mornings?" her eldest daughter, Francesca, asked, pointing to her two younger brothers sitting nearby, smiling.

"How could I forget?" Nonna Maria said. "Gabriel would put a handful of coins in the front pocket of his shirt, while the boys prepared the soap, the razor, and the water."

"My brothers would take turns soaping up my father's face, always getting more soap in his eyes than on his beard," Francesca said. "Every single week, the same thing happened.

"My father would say, 'I don't understand, the beard is on my face, not my eyes,'" Francesca said, laughing as she spoke. "And as he said this, my brothers would take the coins from his shirt pocket and then leave without ever finishing the shave."

Nonna Maria smiled. "Gabriel loved it as much as the boys," she said. "I asked him once, 'Why not just give them the money and save yourself having soap in your eyes every Sunday?' And Gabriel would wrap his arms around me, smile, and say, 'Maria mia, what would the fun in that be?'"

As the hours passed, the plentiful food was replaced by plates filled with fresh pastries and cookies along with pots of espresso and bottles of Sambuca, Limoncello, Fernet-Branca, and Rucolino. An elderly neighbor sat on a bottom step of his home, a lit cigar resting between his feet and an accordion in his hands, and sang a string of old Neapolitan love ballads.

"Days like this bring back so many memories, Nonna Maria," Pepe the Painter said, pulling up a chair and sitting next to her. He was one of her oldest and dearest friends, a widower who sold his paintings on a strip of Corso Vittoria Colonna, next to the Villa Angela. He had a thick mane of white hair and was dressed in a white cotton shirt, sleeves rolled to the elbows, cargo shorts, and brown sandals. "Many meals that we shared with your Gabriel and my wife in our company. So much laughter and, on occasion, a few tears. Back then, in those happy years, we thought we would always think of ourselves as young. But, as is so often the case, the reality of life gets in the way of our dreams."

Nonna Maria looked out at her grown children and their families and at the many friends mingled among them. "I do it for them now," she said. "To give them the same happy memories we once shared. It's all we can do now that we are old, Pepe."

He reached for a carafe of white wine and poured them both a glass. He watched Nonna Maria take a small drink and then rest her glass back on the table. She gazed past the tables, looking out now at the empty street beyond the courtyard. She stayed silent for a few moments and then turned back to Pepe. "I'm going to need your help," she said to him. "I'm glad we were able to enjoy a day like today. Because these next few days are going to be difficult ones."

"Anything I can do, Nonna Maria, I will do," Pepe the Painter said. "Anything."

"This is not like the other times, Pepe, when we stepped in to help our friends," Nonna Maria said. "This time could be dangerous. And as much as I want to help my friends, I also don't want to see any of them hurt. So, before you say yes to anything I ask, give it some thought first."

"I lead a boring life, Nonna Maria," Pepe the Painter said, resting a hand on top of hers. "I do nothing but paint and think about how much I miss having my wife by my side. So a little excitement might do me some good. I will be there for you. I don't need to think about it."

Nonna Maria nodded. "Most of the paintings you sell are of the castle," she said. "Do you spend much time there?"

"I visit two, three times a week," he said. "I've seen it a thousand times down the years, both inside and out. And yet every time I go there, I see something I missed all those other times. It's a magical place and has so many hidden paths, so many secrets within its walls. I could paint it from a hundred different angles and still not capture all that lies within those walls."

"Have you been to the grottoes leading to the caves?" Nonna Maria asked.

"Many times," Pepe the Painter said. "Those sketches are

filled with mystery, a sense of another place, another time far removed from this one. The great Caravaggio himself could not have done justice to those walls and halls and passageways."

"Is there a passageway that leads from inside the castle to any of the cave openings?" Nonna Maria asked.

Pepe the Painter nodded. "It would be difficult to navigate, rocky and very slippery footing," he said. "But yes, you could go from one to the other. Not all of them, of course. But the ones closest to the castle. They were mostly used by the Moors centuries ago as an escape path, back when they held claim to Ischia. The contraband runners, as you know, took the water route to the many caves. The guardians of Ischia used the passageways."

"We might need to make use of both," Nonna Maria said.

"To do what?" Pepe the Painter asked.

"I'm not sure yet," Nonna Maria said. "But they both look like perfect places to set a trap."

19.

THE THICK WOODEN door leading from the foyer into the large room was open, the stucco walls painted dark gray. Tall lamps stood in each corner, their covers matching the color of the walls that surrounded them. A black leather chair sat next to the stone fireplace, and a large couch rested on the other side of the room. There were no windows in the room. An oil portrait of a woman wearing a blue gown and a massive pearl necklace hung directly above the mantel. Nonna Maria stood in the center of the room, her large black tote bag at rest by her foot.

The Pirate had taken her on his motorboat to the borough of Forio, the largest of the six that made up the island of Ischia. He had pulled his boat up to the large dock that led to one of the largest homes Nonna Maria had ever seen. "Those steps over there will lead you to a gate at the rear of the property," the Pirate told her. "Once inside, follow the stone steps to the rear door and let yourself in. The gate and the door won't be locked. He's expecting you. I'll wait for you here."

"I brought him two bottles of wine," Nonna Maria said. "And a platter of stuffed peppers. You should never go into someone's home empty-handed."

"Leave me the wine and take him the peppers," the Pirate

said. "He loves to eat but he doesn't drink much, and it would be a shame to let it go to waste."

"He can save it for when he has company," Nonna Maria said. "You can drink your wine later. *After* you get me back to the port."

It took Nonna Maria a good ten minutes to make her way up the winding and sandy wooden steps to the gate at the rear of the house and another ten to walk the stone path surrounded by manicured bushes and large lemon trees. The house stood high on a bluff overlooking the bay on one end and the center of Forio on the other. Nonna Maria took a few moments to gaze out at the houses and churches dotting the Forio landscape. Unlike the other boroughs of Ischia, many of Forio's structures reflected the two centuries of the Moors' designs and architecture, giving the area a more contemporary look and feel. Don Marco, the priest in her parish of Saint Peter's, once told her, "Ischia has been touched by so many different cultures, from the Greeks to the Romans to the Moors. And the remnants of each culture remain. And our own identity is very much a part of those cultures. Our cuisine, our habits, our dialect, and many, if not all, of the trades practiced here are a mixture of the people who once ruled the island."

Nonna Maria had eased open the front door and stepped into the cool interior of a massive foyer. The large room she now stood in was to the left. She turned when she heard quiet footsteps coming up behind her and found herself standing a few feet from the man known as the Magician.

"Welcome to my home, Nonna Maria," he said.

His voice was soft and warm, and he spoke in the dialect of the island. He was tall with a shaved head that shone in the light from the four floor lamps. He wore dark slacks topped with a long-sleeved black T-shirt and was barefoot. He was muscular, and his skin, from what little Nonna Maria could see in the shadows of the room, was heavily tanned. As he stepped farther into the room, he carried himself with the air of an aristocrat rather than that of a renowned thief.

He reached out a hand to her and smiled. "I've heard so much about you," he said. "Not just from the tales told to me by my friend down at the dock. But from so many others you have helped through the years."

Nonna Maria took his hand into hers and nodded. She took note of the warmth of his hand and the gentle way he held his grip. "And now, here, I come to you asking for your help," she said.

"Please, sit," he said, pointing to the couch. "I would offer you something to drink or eat but have been warned not to do so. The only food or drink you take must come from your own kitchen."

"I don't do it to offend," Nonna Maria said. She picked up her black tote bag and walked over to the couch and sat. "It's a habit of many decades and I'm much too old to change my ways now."

"No offense taken, Nonna Maria," the man said. "I judge only my enemies, never my friends."

Nonna Maria reached into a pocket of her black woolen dress and pulled out a folded piece of paper. "The Pirate has told you about the young woman who came to see me," she said.

The man nodded. "Her grandfather, on his deathbed, made mention of a lost treasure," he said. "What that treasure is and what it's worth was never passed on to the girl."

"No," Nonna Maria said. "But this was. A map. At least a piece of one."

The man walked closer to Nonna Maria and took the folded paper from her. He opened it and studied it for several moments. "What was the name of the young woman's grandfather?" he asked.

"Iacone," Nonna Maria said. "Paolino Iacone. He owned several businesses in the port area. Did you know him?"

"We never met, at least not that I'm aware of," the man said. "We were in competition with one another, back in the years when the Pirate and I worked together."

"He ran contraband," Nonna Maria said. "Same as the two of you."

"To a degree," the man said. "He had a much bigger operation than the two of us. He cast a wider net. We made the bulk of our money moving counterfeit cigarettes, wine, whiskey, and occasionally high-end clothing. He moved those as well, but he also had a higher reach than we did."

"Drugs?" Nonna Maria asked.

The Magician shook his head. "Very few of us back then were interested in getting into that end of the business," he said. "There was plenty of demand for it, much as there is today. But the risks were too great, or at least they were for me and the Pirate. We were making more than enough money with what we were running. If we got caught with contraband cigarettes or wine, the prison sentence would be two years, three at the most. We got caught running drugs, that would have a much different ending. I would be talking to you today from behind the bars of a prison cell."

"Then what did Paolino Iacone move to Ischia that you and the Pirate did not?" Nonna Maria asked.

The Magician glanced down at the map once more, studied it for another moment, and then looked up at Nonna Maria. "Jewels," he said in a low voice. "Paolino Iacone was the best jewel thief in Southern Italy. And none of what he stole those many years ago has ever been found."

20.

CAPTAIN MURINO WALKED past Via Casciaro, cars parked on either side of the street. He was in full uniform, and the day was oppressively warm, but he didn't mind the heat or the blistering rays of the sun.

It was early afternoon, and the streets were free of pedestrians and traffic. The shops were shuttered and the island, with few exceptions, was closed for business for the next few hours. This custom of shutting down all business for four hours in the middle of the day was one Murino had grown used to since he arrived in Ischia. While the practice was observed to a certain degree in the North, it was a time-honored ritual in the South, especially among the locals. The sun-drenched afternoons were a time of relaxation, a break from long hours spent at work or in front of the hot stove of a busy kitchen.

These hours were Murino's favorite time to walk the streets or stop and sit for a time under the shade of a favorite tree, looking out past the tennis courts and the wide expanse of beaches to the quiet bay beyond. This time was usually the most tranquil period of his day. There were no questions to be asked of either victims or suspects, no meetings to be held, no interviews to be conducted. Even the business of crime usually took the hours between 1:30 and 5:30 off on summer days in Ischia.

Murino walked past the closed glass doors of Minicucci's Bar, the smell of fresh-baked pastries still lingering in the air, and started up the sloping curve toward Corso Vittoria Colonna. He moved past the thick rows of pine trees offering some shade from the oppressive heat and gazed at the half-dozen feral cats dozing in a barren lot across the way. He turned at the corner, walking up steps of the Banco di Napoli, across from Saint Peter's Church, and saw two men standing in front of the ATM machine.

At first glance, they didn't appear to be either tourists or locals. They were too well dressed for the quiet hours of the day, and their short-sleeved cotton shirts didn't do much to hide the bulge of weapons resting against their hips. He walked up and stood behind them, watching as one inserted a bank card into the ATM slot and waited. The older of the two turned and smiled at Murino. "It doesn't seem like it wants to give us any of our money," he said to the captain. "Would you happen to know if it's working or not?"

The second man spoke without turning around. "Maybe it's like the rest of this place," he said. "It's taking the afternoon off."

"Do you want to try it?" the older man said to Murino. "Maybe you might have better luck."

"It has a limit as to how much you can take out," the captain said to them, moving his eyes from their faces to their hands. "A two-hundred-and-fifty-euro maximum. If you want more, you will need to wait for the bank to open for business later today."

"That explains it," the older man said. "My friend was looking to take out a thousand euros. To buy his wife a nice gift from one of the jewelry stores up the street."

The younger man turned to face Murino, placing his wallet back in the rear pocket of his tan slacks. "And if she doesn't like it," he said with a smile, "I'll give it to my girlfriend."

Murino smiled at both men and nodded. "Your dialect tells me you're from the North. Florence, most likely," he said to them, stepping a few inches closer. "And your dress tells me you're from one of the working-class neighborhoods. But your hands are not the hands of working men. They're the soft hands of low-level thugs who make a living preying on the working poor of those areas."

"Who are you to talk to us like that?" the older man said. "We don't take that kind of talk from anybody."

"I was making an observation," the captain said.

The older man looked up and down the street. "There's no one around," he said. "It's so quiet. One of us could be left for dead and no one would even notice until a little before five-thirty."

"I could take that as a threat," Murino said. "And if I were to take it as such, I could arrest both of you. It's a federal crime to threaten the life of a carabiniere, even here in Ischia."

"I was making an observation, Captain," the older man said, smiling.

"Not to worry," Murino said. "If you came here today to do me harm, I would have made a better target up the street, in the shadow of the pine trees. But perhaps you were only sent here to be seen. To make me aware you're here. And warn me that, sooner or later, you will move against me. A move I won't see coming."

"If it were up to me, it would be face-to-face," the older man said. His smile replaced by a look of disdain. "Too many of my friends are in prison, courtesy of the carabinieri. Be nice to move the rock from one hand to another."

"I'm sure you both have spent time inside prison walls yourselves," Murino said. "Soon I'll have a better idea who you both are, and which outfit was foolish enough to hire you."

"How will you do that?" the young man said, stepping away from the bank. "We never told you our names."

Captain Murino pointed above his left shoulder. "This whole time, the two of you have been talking in front of that camera above the window there," he said. "That footage will be all I need to identify you and run your sheet." He stared at the men for a moment. "It's a hard business you've chosen to be in. It's even harder if you're stupid. The smart move would be to get out while you still can."

The captain turned and moved down the steps of the Banco di Napoli and back onto Corso Vittoria Colonna.

21.

NONNA MARIA WAS sitting at a back table at La Taverna Verde when Giovanni's white taxi pulled in from the road and parked across the way, next to a small body shop. He waved to her as he opened one of the rear passenger doors and two women stepped out and made their way toward the empty restaurant. They were both wearing the black dresses of a widow, similar in style to Nonna Maria's. In addition, they each had a black shawl covering their head and wore thick-soled black shoes. Giovanni waited by the side of his taxi, wiping his brow with a flowered handkerchief.

The two women stepped up to Nonna Maria's table and looked around. "I have heard this to be a popular restaurant," one of the women said. "I'm surprised to find it so empty."

"It will stay empty for most of the day," Nonna Maria said. "They won't open for business for several more hours. It will give us the time we need to talk."

"Talk about what, Maria?" one of the women asked. "Your friend Giovanni didn't share much information with us."

"Sit down," Nonna Maria said. "There's wine and water and glasses on the table behind you, have as much as you like."

The two women pulled out chairs and sat across from Nonna

Maria. "Before we drink, we need to hear why you asked to meet with us."

"I need your help, Claudia," Nonna Maria said. "And yours as well, Annarella. In truth, I need the help of all the Mourners on the island."

"Help with what?" Claudia asked.

She lifted the black shawl covering her face and leaned closer to the table. She was in her mid-thirties, her dark hair pinned back on both sides, her eyes the color of coal. Her face was thin and as white as any Nonna Maria had ever seen on a woman, a rare sight on an island as drenched with sunshine as Ischia.

"To do what the Mourners have done since World War II," Nonna Maria said. "Save a life."

"Whose life would we be helping to save?" Annarella asked.

"A friend's," Nonna Maria said. "The carabinieri captain, Murino."

"Our small group only helps those who, like us, have suffered the loss of a loved one," Claudia said. "This carabinieri captain has suffered no such loss. And besides, he has his men to protect him. Why would he need any help from the Mourners?"

"These men who are after him have brought harm to many innocent men and women," Nonna Maria said. "You would be saving lives by helping rid us of them."

"We are not a violent group, Maria," Annarella said. "We don't fight with guns or knives. We do our work in the shadows."

"Which is why I have come to you," Nonna Maria said. "I know your history. How you were first formed in the years the Nazis occupied our island. I know about the traps that were set, how their supply lines were disrupted, and their ships damaged. All of it done, as you said, by working in the shadows."

The Mourners were formed in the fall of 1943, organized by seven young widows who had lost husbands and sons in the nightly bombings of Naples, Salerno, and Ischia. Rather than sit back and mourn their losses, they organized a group of women who had suffered similar losses to do what they could to cause chaos for the enemy.

They were a resistance unit of widows, and they planned and executed their work—stealing weapons, raiding food and munitions stations, damaging boats used to transport soldiers from the island to the mainland—under the cover of night.

In time, their activities grew bolder as they set fire to enemy trucks and tanks, sank small boats docked in the harbor, and even helped free locals imprisoned by the enemy.

In the years after the war, the group remained intact to help those who had lost a loved one through any form of injustice. When an older Mourner passed on, she was quickly replaced by a younger one. They were a secretive group, suspicious of outsiders, trusting no one other than those in their own circle.

"That was a long time ago, Maria," Claudia said. "And those original seven Mourners, each having lost a husband or child during the war, have long since passed away."

"I know," Nonna Maria said, looking from Claudia to Annarella. "My mother was one of them. And she helped keep the Mourners together after the Nazis fled. Through the years, they gave shelter to those in need and food to families that had none. And I have heard many stories of how the Mourners, old members as well as new, helped those at risk from money lenders, corrupt landlords, and dangerous men who wished to bring them harm."

"Who are these men looking to bring down the carabinieri captain?" Claudia asked. "And why?"

"The kind of men all of us have seen before," Nonna Maria said. "Willing to do anything to anyone for a price. Many of their own were arrested by the captain and given long prison sentences. Others were killed. They have come here to get revenge."

The two Mourners stayed silent for a few moments. Claudia stood and walked over to a side table and reached for a pitcher of chilled white wine with sliced peaches that had been left by the owner for them to drink and eat. She poured out two glasses, turned and handed one to Annarella, and then sat back down. "There are ten of us now," Claudia said. "Two in our group had sons who were carabinieri and lost both in that tragedy in Sicily four years ago."

Nonna Maria nodded. "I know," she said. "Two others lost husbands in an attack in the North, killed waiting in line for a coffee."

"You've lost family yourself, to disease and to war," Annarella said. "You could be one of our members."

"In my way, I am," Nonna Maria said. "That's why I am here today. I need you to help a good man. A good friend."

Claudia moved her wine glass closer to the center of the table. She put out a hand and reached for one of Nonna Maria's and held it. "We will help your friend," she said. "Any way we can. And we can do it in plain sight. Each of us wears the clothes we wear out of respect for the ones taken from us. But those clothes have a second purpose as well."

Nonna Maria smiled. "No one takes notice," she said. "There are so many wearing the black dress of the widow here in Ischia, no one gives it a thought or a second look."

"To the tourists and many of the locals, we might as well be invisible," Annarella said.

"And an invisible opponent is a dangerous one," Nonna Maria said.

"The Mourners will be there for you," Claudia said. "No one will see us, but we will be there."

"Giovanni will take you wherever you need to go," Nonna Maria said. "He is a trusted friend, and his mother walked alongside mine for many years, doing the work you do today."

Claudia turned and looked across the way at Giovanni's taxi. "It's a shame he has a white van," she said with a smile. "A black one would suit us so much better."

22.

THE BLACK AUDI screeched to a stop on a side street in Cartaromana, less than a quarter of a mile from the home Michelangelo had built for himself centuries earlier. Il Presidente looked at the car, powerful engine idling, gears in neutral, blackout windows hiding the occupants. He was calm, hands at his side, sun at his back. He knew from his years living the life he had led that this was not a situation that would end with bullets. If it were, the car would have slowed, not come to a full stop, and he would already be dead.

Instead, he stood facing the car and waited until the rear door swung open and he heard a voice come at him from the semidarkness of the interior. "Get in," the man sitting in the rear said. "Then close the door behind you."

Il Presidente stared at the open door for a moment, then stepped toward the car and folded his massive frame into the thick black leather of the rear seat and slammed the door shut.

Once inside, Il Presidente turned and faced the man sitting next to him, Cesare Monte. Two men sat in the front, one with both hands on the steering wheel, the second with his body angled so he faced Il Presidente. Both were in their midtwenties and had the expected look the young of their profession required—razor-cut hair, taut and muscular, prepared to do what needed to be done to protect the life of the man sitting casually in the rear seat of the late-model Audi sedan.

"Let's take a tour of the island," Monte instructed the driver. "And keep your eyes on the road. Both of you. While I have a little chat with our guest."

The Audi pulled away from the curb and eased down the empty street, turning right at the corner and making for the outer boroughs of Ischia.

Monte turned toward Il Presidente and folded his arms across his chest. He was dressed in a black button-down shirt, dark slacks, Gucci shoes, and a thin Armani leather jacket. "I heard you wanted to meet with me," he said, his voice soft, his Neapolitan accent thick. "And it has been a long time since I was driven around the island. This way, I get both done at once."

Cesare Monte was the head of the Camorra, the most feared organized-crime outfit in Naples and the surrounding areas. His grandfather had run the syndicate during the black-market years of World War II, and then it fell to his father to rule the outfit. Cesare had been groomed to take over from the time he was a teenager and had been in charge now for more than three decades.

He was in his mid-fifties but looked ten years younger. He had a rich head of dark hair, graying slightly at the temples, and an evenly trimmed salt-and-pepper beard. His eyes were the color of granite and he seldom smiled. He kept his own counsel and was known to be a man of his word, gracious to his few friends and associates and brutal to his many enemies.

"I don't usually meet with just anyone, as you can imagine," Monte said to Il Presidente. "But the stories told about you could fill half a dozen books. And my father always spoke about you with respect. So I thought I'd look for myself and hear you out."

"We have a friend in common, you and me," Il President said.

Monte shrugged. "I would think someone who had been in your line of work couldn't afford to have friends," he said.

"I have only one," Il Presidente said. "Nonna Maria."

"The old widow," Monte said. "If you're going to have only one, you can't do better than Nonna Maria."

"A friend of hers is in trouble," Il Presidente said. "That's the reason I wanted to sit and talk to you."

"Who?"

"His name is Paolo Murino," Il Presidente said. "He's the captain of the carabinieri here in Ischia. There are men on the island who want to kill him. And she will do everything she can to prevent that."

The Audi sedan was passing the massive volcanic mushroom jutting out of the bay at Lacco Ameno. Monte gazed at it for a moment until it passed out of sight and then turned to look at Il Presidente. "I know who he is," he said. "What I don't know is why I should care if a carabinieri captain's life is at risk."

"The men are not part of your organization," Il Presidente said. "And I'm more than certain whoever sent them did not come to you and ask for permission to take out a carabinieri captain."

"Go on," Monte said, staring out the window at the wide expanse of the Bay.

"For the moment, let's put that slight aside," Il Presidente said. "Let's say these men manage to take out the captain. And, whether meaning to or not, bring harm to Nonna Maria. These men, if they survive, head back to wherever they came from and leave you and your organization to face the heat that will come down heavy from the carabinieri, not just from here in Ischia or in Naples, but from everywhere in Italy. And that's not the kind of heat any boss wants coming at them."

"How are you involved in this?" Monte said. "It's not like you to give a second thought to anyone, let alone a member of the carabinieri."

"Normally, I don't," Il Presidente said. "But Nonna Maria will be in the middle of whatever's going to happen. And I care about what happens to her. She's more than my friend. She's become my family."

Monte nodded and stayed quiet for several moments, content to glance at the passing scenery. "How many men were sent down to handle the job?" he asked Il Presidente.

"Four that we know about," Il Presidente said. "They could be hired guns, or they could be decoys, giving time and space until the real shooter is ready to make his move."

"I'm glad you came to me," Monte said. "You're right, I did not sanction anyone from either inside or outside my organization to go after anyone, let alone a carabinieri captain. If you work for me, you know Ischia is off-limits. We vacation here, we don't do business here. Not under my father's rule and never under mine."

"The carabinieri captain has made a home for himself in Ischia," Il Presidente said. "He's engaged, looking to buy a house, and has the respect of many on the island. But earlier in his career, he worked in the North, on streets not as peaceful as ours. Streets run by Guido Ostino."

"Ostino is in prison and the only way for him to get out will be when he's driven through the gates in a coffin," Monte said. "But as long as he breathes, he is still a danger."

"The carabinieri captain was the one who put him in that prison," Il Presidente said. "And he was the one who led the team that took down Ostino's Red Squad. He didn't stop until every one of them was either in prison or in the ground."

Monte turned to face Il Presidente. "They were hit heavy, that's for certain," he said. "But not all of them were taken down. A few went into hiding. Some even came south, looking to join up with other crews."

"Yours?" Il Presidente asked.

Monte shook his head. "I like to sleep at night," he said. "And bringing in a strange face from the North, regardless of reputation, would bring an end to that. I only hire internal. Same as my father did."

"The ones that are here will need to show their hand soon," Il Presidente said. "As it is, they are working at a disadvantage."

"They don't know the island," Monte said. "They are on unfamiliar territory. They don't know the best places to hit and to hide. And they need to figure the best and fastest way to make their run back home. And, unless I'm wrong, they have no one here to help guide them. That fact alone plays in the captain's favor. And yours."

"Unless they already have someone in place here who does know all those details," Il Presidente said. "Someone who has been lying in wait to attack at just the right moment."

"You're working your end alone, as you did when you worked for my father?" Monte asked.

"I was a younger man back then," Il Presidente said. "And a

much more heartless one. Nonna Maria has shown me a better way to live. In our business, however, that change is a weakness. I don't know if I can go back to being the man I once was. But that's what I will do if it means keeping Nonna Maria safe."

"The old woman came to see me not long ago," Monte said. "She did a favor for me, and I did one for her, and we both kept our word. Plus, I liked her. And my father liked her as well. You will not be alone, Il Presidente. On that you have my word."

The Audi sedan came to a stop near the old Roman ruins. Monte reached out a hand and rested it on Il Presidente's left leg. "You have one more battle ahead of you," he said. "Don't worry about not being up to it. You love that old woman, it's easy to see. And love, more than hate or revenge, gives us all the strength we need to win any fight we find ourselves in."

Il Presidente nodded and stepped out of the Audi. He closed the rear passenger door and stood on the empty side street, watching as the car with the Camorra boss in the back seat drove off. He turned and began a slow walk to the port, ignoring the heat of a hot sun and the heavy humidity engulfing him, preparing himself to go up once again against men paid to spill innocent blood.

23.

THE PIRATE EASED the motorboat into the wide mouth of the open cave and turned the engine off. He let the boat idle and float as it eased closer toward the rocks and the opening just to the right of the cave. Nonna Maria sat in the bow of the boat, her hands resting on the wood. She leaned forward, taking in the area, the air cool on her face, the water lapping against both sides of the boat.

"Be careful when you step out of the boat," the Pirate said. "The stones are very slippery. Keep your sandals on and wait for me to get off first. I'll grab hold of you and help you out. And leave the tote bag. You won't need it in there."

The Pirate looped a thick rope around two heavy stones and pulled down on it tight, to make sure it was secure. "Will that be enough to hold it?" Nonna Maria asked. "As you know, I can't swim."

The Pirate smiled and shook his head. "It is hard for me to imagine how anyone born and raised on an island, especially this island, never learned to swim," he said. "How is that possible?"

"My mother needed me to help in the grocery store," Nonna Maria said. "And when I wasn't working there, I was home working in the kitchen or cleaning the house. It was a big family and we all had to do what was asked of us. There wasn't much time left to go to the beach and learn to swim."

"Times were difficult during those years," the Pirate said. "Not just for your family, but for everyone on the island. But still, when you got older, and were engaged to Gabriel, that might have been a good time to spend a day or two at the beach."

"Gabriel was a shepherd," Nonna Maria said, "not a sailor."

"Let's get to it, then," the Pirate said, stepping out of the boat and onto the slippery stones around the cave. "That is, if you still want to go through with this and see the inside of one of the caves."

"I want to see for myself what it's like in there," Nonna Maria said. "Since I was a young girl, I've heard stories about these caves. But I've never been inside one. What better time than now to find out?"

He reached out a hand and helped ease Nonna Maria onto the gray rocks, keeping one arm wrapped around her waist. The Pirate was dressed in his customary red Speedo and bandanna wrapped tight around his head. He had a red scarf tied around his neck and his thick gray hair was combed back and held in place by two red bands. His salt-and-pepper beard was dotted with water, his skin was deeply tanned and lined like an alligator's, and his bare feet handled the slippery surface with an experienced ease.

"The inside of the cave looks dark from here," Nonna Maria said, finding her footing. "Will you be able to make your way once we're inside?"

"I used this cave in the years I was running black-market goods from Naples," the Pirate said. "I practically lived here back then. I know those walls better than I know the waters of the island. I'll have your hand in mine, and that will be all the light you will need."

"And this leads us out where?" Nonna Maria asked.

"These tunnels and curves will take us all the way to Ischia Ponte," the Pirate said. "From here, no more than ten minutes. We'll come out near the entrance to the castle. In my black-market years, I would always come out at night, ease into the crowd enjoying their late-night walk and gelato, my money safely hidden back in the cave, and walk away without any worries or concerns."

"A man wearing only a red bathing suit and a bandanna would be noticed no matter the time of day," Nonna Maria said. "Which tells me you did wear clothes at one point in your life."

The Pirate laughed out loud. "Did I wear clothes?" he said. "Nonna Maria, I was the best-dressed black-market runner in Italy. I kept a trunk full of clothes in one of the side passageways of the cave. I would change out of the dark clothes I needed to wear to avoid detection and come out wearing white linen shirts and cargo shorts and sneakers from America. The ladies noticed me for sure, but never the carabinieri."

"I'm sorry I never got to see you back then," Nonna Maria said, walking gingerly toward the mouth of the tunnel opening. "Other than that night spent with the Baroness, I have never seen you in anything but your current outfit."

"Once I gave up the trade, I took to my motorboat and lived my days and nights in the water," the Pirate said. "I turned my back on the life I led. All I kept was a blanket, a sword, a shirt, a handful of red bandannas and kerchiefs, and the bathing suit. There wasn't much need for anything else."

Nonna Maria reached for one of the Pirate's hands and held it in her own. "Let's go see these tunnels," she said.

The Pirate nodded. "Keep your head low," he said. "And do your best not to bump into the sides, especially when we make the turns. Some of the walls have sharp edges."

They hunched their shoulders and entered the tunnel, turning left at the curved opening. They left behind the warmth and the daylight and quickly felt the cool air and moisture surrounding them. They turned several corners, the passageways growing darker with each step, air cold enough for Nonna Maria to see puffs of her breath ease from her mouth. The Pirate stopped at an intersection between two openings.

"Can you see where we are?" he asked.

Nonna Maria squinted and nodded. "There's one entrance to the left and one to the right," she said.

"If you make the wrong decision which way to go," the Pirate said, "you could be in this cave for days if not weeks trying to make your way out. And this is one of the easiest of the caves. Some of the others are rumored to have traps set in the walls and spread among the rocks."

"What kind of traps?"

"If true, the kind that can keep you locked in until your last breath," the Pirate said.

"How did you know which caves were safe to use and which were a risk?" Nonna Maria asked.

"I didn't," the Pirate said. "And, as far as I know, few of the contraband runners did. In my case, it was pure luck. But the Magician didn't count on luck. He made a study of these caves, read as much as he could about the ones who used them in the past. And then he took the time to explore them. He ran a risk doing that. He could have been trapped in one himself. With him on board, we can safely look for any treasure that may or may not exist within the walls of the caves. The same can't be said by any other treasure hunters."

"Which way?" Nonna Maria said, pointing to openings on either side of a solid wall of stone. "Right or left?"

The Pirate turned to his right and led Nonna Maria into the darkened cave. "This will take us closer to the castle," he said. "The other route leads to a twenty-foot drop down a crater hole."

They made their way slowly through the tight space, the Pirate, despite his bare feet, maneuvering with calm confidence over terrain he had walked on for decades. Nonna Maria was much more cautious, the pain in her damaged right hip amplified by the rugged path, the slippery ground, the walls not always safe to lean on for assistance.

After several more turns, Nonna Maria could see specks of light ahead of them and the muffled sounds of voices and music from above their heads. "We're less than five minutes from the opening by the castle," the Pirate said. "Once we're out in open air and on solid ground, I'll head back through the tunnel and get my boat and head out to sea. And not to worry, I'll keep your tote bag safe."

"I packed something in there for you, for later," Nonna Maria said. "Two bottles of D'Ambra white wine and two red-pepper-and-egg panini."

"I knew you would bring something for me," the Pirate said. "I'll have one of each tonight and save the other two for breakfast in the morning."

"You should have coffee, not wine, with breakfast," Nonna Maria said. "It's better for your stomach."

"That would be true for most people, Nonna Maria," the Pirate said. "But if I'm going to call myself a pirate, then I think it would be best if I lived and ate like one."

They reached the end of one area of the cave, facing an iron ladder wedged into the wall. "This will take us to the top," the Pirate said. "There's a boulder blocking the entrance from view. It's in a place that's shrouded in darkness and too far from the castle steps for anyone to notice."

"And you're strong enough to push aside a boulder?" Nonna Maria asked.

"If it were a real boulder, no," the Pirate said. "We would both be stuck here, shouting for help. But since it is only made to look like a boulder, then we move ahead without any worries."

The Pirate began his climb up the short and rusty ladder, the iron bars turned green from decades of neglect. Nonna Maria followed, gripping the sides of the ladder as she maneuvered up each step. She then waited as the Pirate rested his back against the stone wall and shoved the boulder aside.

"How many know about this passageway?" she asked, slowly making her way to the top step.

"Until today, just two," the Pirate said. "Now there are three."

"Your secret is safe with me," Nonna Maria said.

The Pirate turned and gazed down at Nonna Maria, grasping her hand and helping her up the final few steps. "All our secrets are," he said.

24.

CAPTAIN MURINO WALKED beside his fiancée, Loretta D'Angelo, enjoying a brief interlude from his carabinieri duties. They had been engaged now for three years and were very much in love, so much so that Murino had filed a formal request asking to remain in Ischia until his retirement. It was an unexpected move and came as a bit of a surprise to his superiors, especially given the adrenaline-fueled early years of Murino's career. But the captain felt those years were well behind him now, and he longed for a peaceful life with a loving wife and a family of his own.

They were meant to be wed last summer, but Loretta's father had been ill and in need of surgery, so the couple chose to postpone the event until he was well into his recovery. Now yet another obstacle stood in their way: a threat to Murino's life. And Murino was determined not to proceed with his wedding until his safety and that of his fiancée were assured.

Loretta rested her head on the captain's shoulder as they walked. She was several years younger, in her mid-twenties, tall and slender, with rich strands of thick dark hair, charcoal-colored eyes, and a smile that would warm any young man's heart. She was Ischia born and raised, the youngest of three daughters. Her father owned the pharmacy in the port and her mother worked as a hotel receptionist. Loretta had a contagious laugh, loved to read, and worked as a municipal police officer, assigned to traffic detail in the port and in Ischia Ponte.

They had met at the scene of an accident, and they bonded over their love of books.

A Fiat 500, a mini-taxi, and a Vespa had somehow collided on a narrow street near the entrance to the large bookstore in Ischia Ponte. Such an incident fell under the jurisdiction of the municipal police, and Loretta was the first to respond. She surveyed the scene and was doing her best to calm the tempers of the three agitated drivers.

"It was all his fault," the woman who had been driving the Fiat 500 said, pointing to a teenager in a Billy Joel T-shirt and jeans torn at the knee. She was in her mid-fifties, her tanned face flushed, her beach robe spotted with sweat. "He wasn't looking and ran right into my car. Look at that dent!"

The young man lifted his Vespa from the ground and shook his head. "What dent?" he asked. "You would need a magnifying glass to see any marks on her car. And she failed to mention she was on her cell phone when she turned the corner and rammed into me and my scooter."

An elderly man stood next to the side of his white mini-taxi and lit a cigarette. "You can't put any blame on me," he said. "I wasn't even driving. I stopped here to get a coffee and get out of the sun. How can I cause an accident when I'm not even behind the wheel? If anything, this woman owes me. She hit the scooter and then the rear of her car hit the side of my taxi."

Loretta stood off to the side, taking stock of the situation. She had been working traffic detail for two summers now and these minor incidents were often the ones that consumed the greatest amount of her time. In Ischia, a fender bender ends up being the scene of high drama and theatrics. Loretta had started to enjoy the spectacle, provided there were no injuries. And she always sought to resolve the matter to the contentment of all parties involved.

Captain Murino was coming out of the bookstore, having purchased the latest volume in the Inspector Montalbano series, and turned to look at the unfolding scene, his attention more on the attractive municipal police officer than what appeared to be an incident of little concern.

He walked the short distance to the scene and smiled as he approached Loretta. "It doesn't seem like you need any help," Murino said to her. "But I would be more than happy to assist if you do."

"It seems to be under control, Captain," Loretta said, noticing the bars on his carabinieri uniform. "No one has been injured and the damages are minimal."

"Who is going to pay for the damage done to my car?" the woman standing behind Murino and Loretta shouted. "And now we have the carabinieri with us as well. A few days in one of your cells would teach this young one a lesson he will never forget."

Murino looked away from Loretta and at the angry woman. "No one is going to jail," he said in a calm voice. "And as for the damage done to your car, which to my eye seems like nothing more than a scratch, that can be easily resolved."

"How?" the woman asked.

"Take your car to the mechanic near the carabinieri station," Murino said, "whenever is convenient for you. He will fix it in a matter of minutes and there will be no charge. And the same applies to the gentleman with the mini-taxi. Provided that the municipal officer here agrees with my decision."

"I have no problem with your solution," Loretta said, smiling. "It seems the fastest and best way for all of us to get on with our day."

Captain Murino and Loretta watched with detached amusement as the trio began to untangle and embark on their separate ways, the quick resolution to the matter bringing both their tempers and their voices back to normal levels.

"Thank you for your assistance, Captain," Loretta said. "This is the first time I've had a carabinieri officer stop to help solve a traffic dispute."

"You had the situation well under control," Captain Murino said. "I just happened to be coming out of the bookstore and stopped by out of curiosity more than anything."

Loretta glanced at the book in Murino's hand. "I see you're a fan of Camilleri," she said. "He's one of my favorites."

"I've read all the Montalbano novels," Murino said. "But sadly, this is the last. He died soon after he finished it. I'll have to discover another author to spend my free hours with."

"I could recommend a few to you," Loretta said.

"That would be helpful and much appreciated," Murino said. "And if you like, it might be pleasant to discuss your recommendations over a coffee and a pastry."

Loretta smiled. "I would like that," she said. "But the coffee, the pastry, and the book recommendations will have to wait. I'm on duty for several more hours."

Captain Murino nodded, reached into his jacket pocket, and pulled out a cell phone. He pressed a button, and his call was picked up on the second ring. "Franco, it's Murino," he said into the receiver. "Patch me through to the duty officer of the municipal police." While he waited, he rested the phone against his leg, turned to the young officer and said, "I'm afraid I neglected to ask your name."

"Loretta," she said. "Loretta D'Angelo."

The duty officer came on the line and again Murino raised the phone to his ear. "Buona giornata, Sergeant," he said. "This is Captain Paolo Murino of the carabinieri. I will require the help of one of your officers currently on duty. Loretta D'Angelo. Most likely for the rest of the day. I would like you to arrange for another officer to take over her shift."

Murino listened for a moment. "I'm afraid I can't answer that, Sergeant," he said. "What I can tell you is it is official carabinieri business and her help will go a long way in resolving an important matter. She has the knowledge and expertise that are required."

Murino held the receiver for another moment and then ended the call. He turned to Loretta standing there with a bemused expression on her face. "For the next few hours, at least, you're assigned to me," he said to her. "Which means our next stop will be at Café Vittoria. I stop there nearly every day. I think it would be a perfect place for us to drink coffee, eat a fresh-baked pastry, and talk about our favorite books. Or anything else you would like to discuss. Unless you have another café you prefer?"

Loretta shook her head and smiled at Captain Murino. "Café Vittoria is a great choice," she said.

25.

"I THINK IT might be best if you left Ischia for a few days," Murino said to her now. He gazed at her, the sun at her back, her rich strands of hair folding along the sides of her face. He was always struck by her natural beauty, her smile and easy manner, her warmth and goodness. He had never felt this much love for anyone in his life, and entangled in that love was a constant and interminable fear that he would lose her, that the dangers he faced would bring her harm. It was a feeling he could not shake. Threats to his life were by now second nature to him, some easier to shrug away than others, always with the awareness that it was all part of being a member of the carabinieri.

"I don't want to leave you," Loretta said. "Especially not now. I couldn't live with myself if something horrible happened to you and I could have been here to prevent it. You must let me help you, not send me away."

"These are dangerous men, Loretta," the captain said. "And while I love you for wanting to help me, they're ruthless and will show no mercy. You would be no match for them, and I couldn't stand to see you in harm's way."

"That's because you think of me as only a traffic officer," Loretta said.

Captain Murino shook his head. "No," he said. "I think of you as the woman I love. The one I want to spend the rest of my life with, raise a family with, and grow old with, both of us reading the latest thrillers and mystery novels together."

"Then let me help you, Paolo," Loretta said. "I know this island better than these men who will come here to do you harm. I have friends in every borough. And while the municipal police don't make criminals tremble as much as your unit does, they can be a help, especially here on Ischia. Unlike your men, most of whom are new to the island, the members of the municipal force were born and raised here, and that's something you should take advantage of. You should not go into this alone."

"I won't be alone," Captain Murino said. "Even though I would prefer that no one else be involved. But whether I want Nonna Maria and her friends to help or not, there isn't much I can do to stop them. They've already made up their minds."

"So have I, Paolo," Loretta said. "I know you like to go your own way, and you did for many years, especially working in the North. But it's different for you here. You have made this island your home, and many of the locals have grown to care about you. Nonna Maria thinks of you as another one of her sons. They care because they love you. And none of them love you as much as I do. So, sorry, Captain, I'm not going anywhere."

Captain Murino turned and embraced Loretta, holding her close, resting the side of his face against the nape of her neck. "I could have you brought in on some trumped-up charges, you know," he whispered. "Nothing serious. Just something that would keep you out of the way."

Loretta eased away from his grip and smiled at Murino. "You can try," she said. "But then my father would call his dear friend

Nonna Maria and she would have me out long before your men could finish the paperwork."

Captain Murino nodded and raised his hands in mock surrender. "Maybe I should just sit this one out," he said with a smile. "Let you and Nonna Maria deal with these men."

"They wouldn't stand a chance," Loretta said.

She took Murino's hand into hers and they continued their walk, finding peace and comfort in the quiet of the moment. Yet one more couple in love on the island of Ischia.

26.

F. EMMITT SHAW stood on the upper deck of the tour boat *Anna Lauro,* his tattooed arms resting on the white railing. He was a large, barrel-chested man in his late fifties, his skin lined and darkened from decades spent under hot suns as he journeyed around the world in search of undiscovered treasures. In his many years of searching, Shaw had managed to make only two discoveries. The first, a chest filled with ancient coins dating back centuries, found in the wreckage of a seventeenth-century vessel off the Barbados coast, earned him a feature article in a now-defunct historical magazine.

The second, dozens of rusty iron casks filled with gold coins and jewels found in the dark underbelly of the Atlantic Ocean, earned him a small fortune.

The discovery gave Shaw the luxury of time as he continued his obsessive hunt for treasures long buried and forgotten. It also enabled him to stay a step ahead, allowing him to follow his own whims and not dash about hunting down clues for every rumored lost pot of gold.

Frederick Emmitt Shaw was born into a family of treasure hunters. His father, Clayton Shaw, spent his entire adult life in search of the rumored billions said to have been lost by numerous explorers from centuries past, from Magellan to da Gama and stretching as far back in time as the era of the Vikings. Clayton left his native Australia penniless and filled with hope. He always returned riddled with debt and desolate. His long-suffering and all-too-patient wife, Elena, kept the family of two daughters and a son afloat by working herself nearly to death in Melbourne as a court stenographer in the criminal division by day and freelance editing technical pamphlets at her kitchen table late into the evening.

Emmitt Shaw was not going to repeat either his father's errors in judgment or his hard-drinking ways. Nor would he glean his information from idle bar talk or rumors picked up in internet chat rooms. The only gold to be mined from such areas would be that of a fool. Instead, Emmitt Shaw decided that knowledge and connections would be what would eventually lead him to discovering the fortunes that had always eluded his father's grasp.

From a young age, Emmitt Shaw devoured any books he could find, both fiction and historical, about lost treasures and antiquities. He spent hours in museums and libraries and in front of his computer studying maps of the routes taken by explorers, from the ancient to the modern. He studied the weather patterns of the waters that were traveled and the lands that were crossed. He built a network of like-minded treasure seekers and exchanged data and theories and argued over the validity of any possible discovery.

Emmitt Shaw—he abandoned the Frederick while still in his teens—also realized, as his father never did, that he would need benefactors to fund his journeys. So, much as he made it his business to know as much about lost treasure as he could, he began to research the names and histories of the few rich donors interested in the discovery of any lost items of great value. These men or women could supply him with the tools and the crew he would need to finance his often-months-long travels.

As he stood on the upper deck of the tour boat, gazing out at the sparkling waters surrounding the island of Ischia, Emmitt Shaw was in his third decade as a treasure hunter. These days, he sought his adventures more out of curiosity than financial need, more for the thrill of the discovery than for the value of the haul. He never married or lived in any one place for more than five years, spending more time at sea or in the middle of a desert than he ever had in any home of his own.

Emmitt Shaw was a loner who worked with a small but trusted crew of fellow hunters, his journeys often financed by an investment banker's widow living in Madrid. She loved his sense of adventure and trusted he would not abuse her riches. He loved that she asked relatively few questions, was knowledgeable about lost artifacts, and understood the odds and the risks involved in any hunt.

When he made his discovery in 2009, the coins and jewels he brought to the surface were worth an estimated 750 million euros. In return for the full value of the discovery, the coins and jewels were delivered to the Italian government since they were determined to be Italian in provenance. The coins and jewels were then parceled out to several museums throughout the country. Shaw gave his benefactor half the value of his reward. The rest he deposited in a French bank and continued living the only life he had ever wanted.

A woman came up to Shaw, stood to his right, and gazed out at the waters. "You were right about this island," she said in a smoke-stained voice. "It is more than beautiful."

Shaw nodded. "It's one of the few places I've seen in life where I could drop anchor and live out the rest of my days," he said. "There's a soothing calm to its beauty. That's something that restless souls like us require."

"That it has," the woman said. "Though I'm not quite ready to drop anchor and call it a day. But the question remains: Is there lost treasure to be found here?"

"That's still an open question, Barbara," Shaw said. "There have been many rumors about this island across the years, and none of them have turned out to be true. Yet the talk persists, and the chatter has picked up considerably in the last few days."

"But you've never been one to give much weight to chatter," Barbara said with a smile. "Why start now?"

"Maybe because this time, they might be on to something," Shaw said.

"What makes you think that?" Barbara asked, brushing strands of her red hair away from her eyes. She was tall and slender, her body more muscle than bone thanks to daily ten-mile runs and a yoga obsession. She was born in a small Ohio town and raised in a working-class section of Cleveland. She married and divorced at an early age, took her settlement, and headed out to sea, eventually landing a job with a cruise ship line.

She had always been an avid reader, switching easily from a Jane Austen novel to a Jack Higgins thriller, finding satisfaction in both. But it was during that first cruise, hunting through the ship's library, that Barbara Fay discovered the works of Patrick

O'Brian and Rafael Sabatini. O'Brian fed her love of the sea, and Sabatini made her want to explore the world and seek a life filled with action and adventure. A chance encounter with Emmitt Shaw in a library map room in Lisbon, during the last day of a forty-eight-hour cruise ship layover six years ago, allowed her a chance to seek all that and more.

"A man named Paolino Iacone died and was buried here not long ago," Shaw said. "This island was where he made his home and he never left it, at least not during the last fifteen years of his life."

"Was he someone you knew?"

"We never met," Shaw said. "But I heard a great deal about him down the years. He kept to himself mostly, house and family sort of thing, and there was precious little written about him. But he was truly a master of his profession."

"Was he a treasure hunter?" Barbara asked.

Shaw turned and looked at her, the dormant volcano of the island hovering in the distance over her shoulder. "Better even than that," he said. "Paolino Iacone was a man who hid treasure. Or so the tales about him tell us."

"He was a thief," Barbara said. "And he hid his stolen goods on this island. Is that where you're going with this?"

Shaw nodded. "More or less," he said. "He kept a low profile, and there are few on Ischia who are even aware of his reputation. He didn't live a rich lifestyle, kept his ways simple, and stayed under the radar. There was never anything for the police, or the Rome Art Squad, who investigate high-profile thefts, to corner him on."

"How did he off-load the jewels he stole?"

"That's the beauty of it," Shaw said. "He never once tried to sell what he took. Which can mean only one thing if you take it to its logical conclusion."

"He hid them," Barbara said.

"Exactly," Shaw said, turning once again to face the water and gaze out at the mouth of the open caves the tour boat passed. "And if that's true, what better hiding place than the caves he knew so well?"

"At least that helps to explain why you asked me to meet you here in Ischia," Barbara said.

"That's one reason, for certain," Shaw said.

"There's a second?"

"Yes," Shaw said, moving slowly away from the railing and walking toward the steps leading down to the main cabin. "The pasta puttanesca made here in Ischia is said to be the best in the world. That alone would make it a journey worth the taking."

27.

NONNA MARIA HANDED an apron to each of the three grand-daughters gathered in her kitchen. "Put these on," she told them. "They will help keep your clothes clean while we prepare the pies."

The three girls placed the openings over their heads and the oldest, Isabella, tied the string around her waist and then did the same for the other two.

"What are we making, Nonna?" Laura asked. She was eight and was wearing a light blue T-shirt with ISCHIA stenciled in white across the front and a pair of white shorts and Nike sneakers that glowed whenever she took a step.

"We're going to start with pizza Margherita," Nonna Maria told them. "You've all had one, I know. But this will be the first time you will make one of your very own."

Nonna Maria was standing in front of her dining room table. It was filled end to end with rolling pins, pizza dough, carafes of water, three boxes of white flour, cans of San Marzano tomatoes, three large fresh buffalo mozzarellas, a pile of garden-fresh basil and assorted spices, and canisters of olive oil. There was also a large pot of espresso and a cup for her and three glasses and a bottle of chilled mineral water for the girls.

Nonna Maria handed each of her granddaughters a thick wooden cutting board and watched as they each took a place around the table and rested their board in front of them. She gave each of them a rolling pin and placed a large mound of dough on their boards. She sprinkled a handful of white flour on top of the boards, the very same ones she had used to cook with her own children decades earlier.

She reached for the bottle of chilled mineral water and filled the three glasses and placed one in front of each girl. "Drink it if you're thirsty," she said to them. "And if you're not, then wait until the dough is spread out and pour some of it in the center."

"Who showed you how to make pizza, Nonna?" Anna Maria asked. She was seven, with thick sandy-blond hair held in the back by a multicolored ribbon. She had her mother's nervous energy and her father's emerald-green eyes. She could spend hours working on a thousand-piece jigsaw puzzle and would laugh at the silliest antics of her older brothers and uncles.

"When I was your age, it was my Nonna," she said. "Then, as I got older, I made them with my mother or with my sisters. And then, even later, with your mothers and cousins and aunts. But it was my Nonna who told me the stories that go with the pizza. And those stories are as important as the pie."

"I know that the pizza we're going to make is named after the lady who used to be our queen a long time ago," Isabella said. "My mother told me she came to Naples, had her first pizza, and liked it so much that the men there who made them named the pie in her honor."

"That part's true," Nonna Maria said. "But the pie they made in her name also did honor to our country. Look at what we have around the table and what we will put on our pie. Mozzarella, basil, San Marzano tomatoes. One white, one green, one red. Just like the colors of our flag."

"Do the pies in other countries do the same?" Isabella asked. "America's colors, I think, are red, white, and blue. I don't know anything that's blue that would look good on a pie."

"Blueberries," Laura said with a wide smile. "I love blueberries. Maybe that's what they put on their pie in America."

"I hope not," Anna Maria said. "That would taste awful."

Nonna Maria reached for a lump of dough and shrugged. "I don't know what they do in other countries," she said. "But I do know, little one, that fruit belongs in a bowl and in pies made in a bakery. But never on pizza. That would be as bad as putting grated cheese on pasta with clam sauce."

Nonna Maria began to knead the dough with both hands, running it up and down on the tabletop, occasionally pounding at it with a closed fist. "Do with your dough what I'm doing with mine," she told her granddaughters. "Roll and spread and pound until your dough is flat. As it spreads out, pour some water on it and sprinkle in some of the flour. If you're having trouble, let me know and I'll come around and help you."

"Will we get to flip the dough in the air and catch it, Nonna?" Anna Maria asked. "Like I see Pino do in his pizzeria?"

"He catches the dough with a closed fist," Isabella said, "and then tosses it up again. It goes so high, sometimes I think it will reach the ceiling."

"Pino loves to put on a show," Nonna Maria said. "And he's very good at tossing the dough. But he's not as good as his father. Not yet. His father would have his guitar player play and sing a song while he flipped the dough in the air, and he would not stop until the song ended. I used to take my children to see him when they were your ages. They loved watching Pino's father toss the dough almost as much as they loved the pizza he served."

Nonna Maria stood back, wiped her hands on the apron tied around her waist, and took a sip of coffee. She watched as each girl wrestled with the dough, struggling to make it flat, their hands, faces, and aprons covered with flour and specks of dough and streaked with drops of water. "Anyone need any help?" she asked. "If not, I'll go downstairs and get the wood fire started."

"It's easier to eat it, Nonna, than it is to make it," Anna Maria said. She wiped strands of hair from her eyes, half her face covered with white flour.

"You're doing good work, little one," Nonna Maria said. "And the hard work will make you enjoy the pizza you make even more."

"Can I stop for a while, Nonna?" Anna Maria asked. The youngest of the trio looked as exhausted as she felt and had more flour on her arms, face, hair, and apron than she did on the dough.

"Why don't you all sit back and relax for a while," Nonna Maria said. "And watch me make the pies. That might be a better way for you to learn how to make them. You'll see how much oil and spices are needed and how much of the San Marzano tomato sauce must be spread over the dough."

"And how much basil and how much of the mozzarella to add on top," Anna Maria said.

"Then we'll put the pies in the wood-burning oven," Nonna Maria said. "And then we'll sit together while you eat the pies named after a queen."

"Was Queen Margherita the first one to eat a pie?" Laura asked.

"One of the first, but not the first," Nonna Maria said. "Pizza is a simple food and costs very little to make. It's food for workers with not much money and even less time."

"So, who was the first to make pizza?" Isabella asked.

"I don't know the name," Nonna Maria said. "But I'm pretty sure it was a man or a woman who worked long hours and had just enough money to buy bread, oil, and either salami or cheese. And with that, along with a hot fire, a family was fed."

"And pizza was made," Isabella said.

Nonna Maria nodded. "It's the simple things that always last forever," she said. "And are always remembered. It was as true then as it is today."

28.

THE YOUNG CARABINIERI officer sat in a soft leather chair across from Captain Murino's desk. He was in his mid-twenties, his light brown hair hanging loose, a bit longer than regulation required. He was clean-shaven, with clear blue eyes and an affable manner. He had been stationed in Ischia just shy of six months and had thus far blended in smoothly with the other officers under Murino's command. And while he had quickly adapted to the rhythm and pace of the island, he had not yet mastered the Ischia dialect, exposing his Northern Italian upbringing each time he spoke to a local.

His name was Nicola Spazzi, and his transfer from Florence to Ischia had been formally accepted by Captain Murino after receiving glowing recommendations from his commanding officer, a carabiniere who had served alongside Murino during his years of service in that city. Spazzi was to be stationed in Ischia for a year, with a possibility to extend the stay an additional six months.

Murino had kept a close eye on young Spazzi, as he did with any of the officers who were temporarily assigned to the island. He noted how he handled the few cases that fell his way, most of them minor business disputes involving nonpayment for services and physical threats and the rare but occasional robbery or street mugging. He was always on time with his reports, written in a concise and detailed way, and though friendly, kept to himself and did not socialize with any of the other members of the unit.

Despite the good behavior and positive feedback from the other officers, there was something about Nicola Spazzi that troubled Murino. He couldn't pinpoint it or explain it, but he couldn't shake the feeling that the young officer was not all that he seemed. Murino had gone over all Spazzi's work papers, from his initial application to the academy to his impressive arrest records in his two prior assignments—Verona and Florence. His school records, his working-class family background, his volunteer work in impoverished areas of both cities, his care for a disabled relative, his eagerness to take on extra duties and responsibilities, all pointed to a young officer with a bright future ahead of him. And yet there was something not quite right with officer Nicola Spazzi. Captain Murino often thought back to the words of his mentor, Marshal Ranieri Cortono. "If the picture presented to you looks too good to be true," he would often say to his pupils, "then you can trust that very little, if any part of it, is true at all."

"You asked to see me, Nicola?" Captain Murino asked. He had decided early in his tenure to dispense with most formalities while in the office, though expecting them to be observed out in public. He thought it made for a more trusting and welcoming work environment if the men and women under his command felt more comfortable and less constrained.

"Yes, sir," Nicola said. "I have come to offer my help in any way I can. Either on duty or off."

"Help in what way?" Murino asked.

"It is not a well-kept secret, sir," Nicola said. "There are men either coming to Ischia or having already arrived in Ischia who wish to do you harm. I would like to help you to bring these men down."

Murino stared at Spazzi for a moment. "This information is known by some of the more senior officers stationed here," he said. "But those discussions weren't meant to be shared with any of the junior staff, and I was assured they were not."

"It wasn't mentioned to me by any other member of the staff, sir," Spazzi said.

"Then how did you learn of the situation?" Murino asked.

"I still maintain a number of street sources in Florence," Spazzi said. "I thought it would be best to have them keep me informed, since sooner or later I'll be stationed back there. My information came from those sources. As you know better than anyone, a street informant can be more valuable to a carabinieri officer than a loaded weapon."

"And what did your informants tell you about these men that allegedly are coming to Ischia?" Captain Murino asked. "Or, as you implied, may already be here?"

"They didn't have to tell me, sir," Spazzi said. "I was able to piece it together on my own."

"And what were you able to piece together?"

"I have studied your career, sir," Spazzi said. "You are one of the reasons I wanted to become a member of the carabinieri. I've followed all your cases, especially the one involving the members of La Squadra Rossa, starting with the takedown of Guido Ostino. You helped wipe out an entire criminal organization. You went up against a gang that was feared not only by the citizens of the city, but by many in our own profession. It was said that Ostino and his crew owned everyone there was to be owned in Florence, from merchants to bankers to judges and the upper tiers of every police department, from municipal to federal. But still you went against them and defeated them. That's why I'm sitting here across from you, and that's why I want to offer my help."

"That was a long time ago, Nicola," Captain Murino said. "Ostino, as you no doubt are aware, is behind bars, and there he will stay until the time comes for Last Rites to be performed. And if there are any members of his Squad left at all, they have long ago lost their iron grip on that city."

"But even behind the bars of a cell, Ostino still has the power to pass down orders," Spazzi said. "And there will still be those willing to carry those orders out. How many remains unknown to us. But we both know that even one is one too many."

"I appreciate your kind words and your concern," Murino said. "But since you seem to have been such a devoted follower of my career in the North, you are aware I work best when I work with as little outside interference as possible. It was true in the North and it is equally true here in Ischia."

"But, sir, with all due respect," Spazzi said, moving closer to the captain's desk, both hands at rest on the top of the thick brown wood, "you had a small team of men and women under your command in Florence, each committed to bringing an end to Ostino's Squadra Rossa. And here in Ischia, these past few summers, you've worked several of your cases together with a local widow. Now, her knowledge and familiarity with the island may have been useful to you on those occasions, but when confronted by men like the ones taking their orders from Ostino, a local widow will be of no help to you. That much I do know."

Captain Murino smiled and sat back in his leather chair, rocking it gently back and forth. "That's because, Nicola, you don't know Nonna Maria as well as I do," he said. "Let's just say that anyone who underestimates Nonna Maria's abilities does so at their own peril."

"So, you're rejecting my offer to help you?" Spazzi asked.

"Not exactly," Murino said. "I would like you to continue to monitor your contacts in the North. Pass on to me what they hear, see, and know. There must be a middleman between Ostino and the men who wish me harm. He's a survivor and has a jungle animal's cunning, and he would not risk making direct contact with anyone to whom he would give a kill order. It would be good to know the name of that middleman. If you can get that to me, you will have done me a great service."

"I will ask my informants, sir," Spazzi said.

Captain Murino nodded. "Many of the men and women assigned to Ischia seem pleased by the assignment," he said. "They see it as a nice break from the hectic pace of the cities where they were previously stationed. But I have had the feeling, since you first arrived, that you cannot wait until your duties here are done. You appear anxious, thirsting for excitement beyond what the island offers."

"I like it here, sir," Spazzi said. "What's not to like? A beautiful island with much to see and even more to do. But I do admit that at times I miss the energy and the vitality of a big city."

"By that, I take it, you miss the criminal activity," Captain Murino said. "Of which there is very little here in Ischia."

Nicola Spazzi smiled. "I must confess, sir," he said, "I do miss that part of my life. I miss that part very much."

Nicola pushed his chair back, stood, saluted Captain Murino, and walked quietly out of the office, closing the wooden door as he left. Murino turned his leather chair around and gazed out the large open bay window that dominated the rear of his office. He saw Nicola step out of the carabinieri station house and watched as the young man pulled a cell phone from the front pocket of his uniform jacket and began to speak into it. He waited until the officer had turned the corner on Via Casciaro before he closed his eyes and rested his head against the soft leather. He stayed that way for several minutes and then he opened his eyes and stood, walking from the chair to the open window, his hands wedged deep into his uniform pockets.

Murino now knew what had troubled him about Nicola Spazzi. The young man had shown his true self during their meeting, briefly lowering the mask that had concealed his identity. It took mere seconds and only a few words for Captain Murino to know.

He finally grasped what had eluded him these past six months. It wasn't Spazzi's relaxed manner blending uncomfortably with his often-dour attitude. It wasn't even his preference for avoiding the company of his fellow officers while off duty. Or that for such a young officer, he sometimes came off as moody and arrogant. In the long run, none of those traits on their own mattered. But collectively, they painted an entirely different portrait than the one Nicola was so very eager to present.

It was a portrait not of a young and ambitious officer eager to rise through the carabinieri ranks.

It was the portrait of a young and ambitious criminal eager to rise through the ranks of organized crime.

Nicola Spazzi was not in Ischia to help save Captain Paolo Murino's life.

Nicola Spazzi was in Ischia to help end it.

29.

NONNA MARIA SAT at a back table at Eden, a restaurant in Ischia Ponte. It overlooked the castle and the crystal waters of the bay, the islands of Capri and Procida visible in the distance. It could be accessed only by motorboat, a free transport supplied by the owner of the restaurant.

Nonna Maria was sitting next to Rita, both facing the view, across from the Pirate and the Magician. In the center of the table, encircled by bottles of mineral water and white wine and multiple glasses, was Paolino's map. The parchment was worn and tattered, the lines faded and ill-defined, arrows and circles and words written in an ink aged by the passage of decades. "Your grandfather had many enviable talents," the Magician said to Rita. "Preserving a map, however, was not one of them."

"The sketches of the caves resemble those on the far end of Barano," the Pirate said. "The ones by the rock formations that look like an elephant's tusks."

"They are also among the deepest of the Ischia caves and the hardest to enter and exit," the Magician said. "That would make them an ideal place to hide pretty much anything of value."

"Why would my grandfather go to such trouble?" Rita asked. "If he did have something he didn't want anyone to see, then why not a safe deposit box at a bank, or even the safe he kept at home?"

The Pirate exchanged a look with the Magician, but both stayed silent. It was not their place to tell Rita the truth about her grandfather, and neither was it the time.

"As we get older, we do many things for many reasons, Rita," Nonna Maria said. "And not all that we do may make much sense, especially to those much younger. But if Paolino went to the trouble to hide what he meant for you to have in the caves and left a map behind to guide you, he probably had good reason to do so."

"Do you know if anyone other than Paolino and yourself has seen this map?" the Magician asked Rita. "Or if he ever made mention to a friend, a relative, a doctor about hiding anything in the caves?"

Rita shook her head. "Not that I'm aware of," she said. "He was a private man and kept to himself mostly. He had some friends, but not ones he would confide in. And our relatives have either died or moved off the island. Except for me, he was alone."

The Pirate reached for a bottle of wine and took a long drink from the bottle. "They make glasses for a reason," Nonna Maria said, pushing a wine glass in his direction.

"None that have ever made any sense to me," the Pirate said.

The Magician picked up the sheet of paper and held it closer to his face. He studied it for several moments and then placed it back in the center of the table. "If I may, what do you think your grandfather left for you in one or more of these caves?" he asked Rita. "What does this notion of a lost treasure mean to you?"

"I'm not sure," Rita said, raising a hand to shield her eyes from the sun. "I've heard the rumors about my grandfather, about the secret life he led. And the way he truly earned his money. But those rumors died out over the years, and I never did give them much attention. It was the idle talk of men sitting in a piazza with little else to do."

"But the map might make you think there is some weight to those rumors?" the Magician said.

"That's one part of it," Rita said.

"What's another?" the Pirate asked.

"Neither one of you would be sitting here with me if you didn't think what my grandfather hid was worth finding," Rita said. "Men like you don't waste time on rumors. You both knew him, maybe you even worked with him. That I don't know and don't need to know. But now I do think there was some truth behind the stories about him."

"Those tales were heard by many people," Nonna Maria said. "Many here on Ischia. And many in other places. Rumors have their way of making themselves heard, no matter where you rest your head."

"Which means what?" Rita asked.

"Which means we are not the only ones who will be out looking for a lost treasure," the Magician said. "The word has no doubt already spread. That is an inevitable by-product of the trade."

"There are no guidebooks or want ads that tell you about a lost treasure," the Pirate said. "Information is passed from one mouth to another, from one city to another, from one doorway to another. Then it is up to the hunter, the pirate, or the mercenary to determine whether the hunt is worth it."

"What makes them decide if it's worth it?" Rita asked.

"Instinct, most of the time," the Magician said. "The reliability of the ones who pass on the information is also a factor. And where the lost treasure is said to be located is also telling."

"But you have your grandfather's map, which gives you an advantage over the ones who may come looking," Nonna Maria said, reaching over and patting Rita's hands. "And you have friends on your side who know those caves and passageways better than anyone, aside from Paolino."

"All that is true," the Magician said. "But what we don't know worries me much more than what we do know."

"What don't we know?" Rita asked.

"How well funded those coming in search of treasure will be, for one," the Magician said. "This is not a poor man's business. It costs money to look for what's lost. Equipment, men, supplies, a place to stay. Many hunters have benefactors. Others borrow in return for handing over a cut of their find to their lenders. It's a passion, but it is also a business, like any other."

"But what if there is nothing to be found?" Rita asked. "What if my Nonno's idea of a lost treasure will be of value only to me?"

"It's a risk," the Pirate said. "But for the ones who make hunting for lost treasure their business, it is a risk worth taking."

"I don't have the kind of money I imagine it will take to pay for what you might need to go looking for Paolino's lost treasure," Rita said.

"They have everything they both need," Nonna Maria said. "There is no need for you to worry."

Rita stayed silent for several moments. Then she looked at both the Pirate and the Magician. "Why are you helping me?"

she asked. "It could be a complete waste of time. And if you're right about others who will be coming to Ischia looking for what my grandfather hid, then it could be dangerous as well. So, why bother?"

"Because I miss the hunt," the Magician said. "I didn't think I did. I have made a good life for myself here on Ischia and I long for nothing. But then Nonna Maria came to see me and told me your story. Once I heard it, I knew it would be something I simply couldn't resist."

"I want to help," Rita said. "It's not right that you take all the risks, and that if there is indeed something of value to be found I'm the one who gets to keep it."

The Magician folded the paper map and put it into the pocket of his black short-sleeved shirt. Then he and the Pirate both moved away from the table and smiled at Rita and Nonna Maria. "Let's see if we can find whatever it was Paolino managed to hide in those caves," the Magician said. "Until we know that, there is nothing for us to discuss."

The Magician and the Pirate walked toward the stone steps leading down to the nearby dock and the waiting motorboat.

"The Magician and the Pirate are our friends," Nonna Maria said to Rita. "Make no mistake on that. They will never betray us. But also never forget how they once made their living. They were both very good at what they did. Much the same way Paolino was very good at what he did. And just like your grandfather, they never did any work for free. I would not expect them to change their ways now."

"So, they are thieves, too," Rita said.

"Yes," Nonna Maria said with a smile. "But they are *our* thieves."

30.

CAPTAIN MURINO KICK-STARTED his Motoguzzi 999 motorcycle and made a sharp turn out of carabinieri headquarters, zooming down the empty side streets. He was out of uniform, dressed in jeans, black button-down shirt, thin leather jacket, and the new pair of sneakers Loretta had bought for him earlier in the week. He was wearing a black helmet with the visor down, and a pair of black leather gloves.

He skirted patiently through the port traffic, swung the bike past a slow-moving bus, and began the climb toward the outer boroughs of the island. After a long day behind a desk, handing out assignments and filling out paperwork, Murino loved nothing better than to take his bike out and head up toward the clean air of the Ischia mountains. He would often go as far as Serrara Fontana and the D'Ambra vineyards, stopping long enough to take in the sun setting just beyond the boundaries of the bay. Those moments on the road or sitting on a boulder and surrounded by long rows of slowly maturing grapes offered a relaxing balm to the stresses of his day. This was his form of therapy, meditative moments spent in a peaceful and serene setting, the pleasure of the open road waiting to complete his calming circle.

Murino was stretched out on a large rock, his helmet resting by his right foot, an empty plastic Acqua Panna bottle curled in his left hand, when he first heard footsteps making their way across the lanes. He kept his eyes closed and listened. The movement was to his left, a few rows behind where he was situated, and there were no sounds other than heel against dust and legs and shoulders brushing against the vines.

He eased his right hand off his chest and twisted his body to reach for the weapon he kept tucked into his jeans. Then he took slow, deep breaths and waited until the footsteps drew closer.

Murino caught the figure moving in the shadows out of the corner of his eye. He rolled off the boulder and landed on his feet, his weapon in both hands, legs crouched. A man stepped out from behind a row of vines, aimed a Baretta at Murino, and fired off two quick rounds. Both bullets zinged past Murino, ripping into a thick row of hedges. The man was wearing a blue T-shirt stained through with sweat. Murino held his position, waiting for the second man to make his move. He was somewhere off to his right, on the opposite side of the first shooter, lying between the vines, his weapon aimed at Murino. The captain caught the movement of vine leaves to his right and fired three rounds in that direction. The first two sent several small rocks hurtling and kicked up a mound of dust. The third went deep into the grove, missing its mark.

Murino stood up, his gun held out in front of him, and moved in the direction of the first shooter, shifting his weapon from side to side, looking to shoot at the first sign of movement. He stopped when he heard the shooter to his left running through the grapevines and deeper into the valley, farther away from Murino. The second shooter fired off two more rounds, both flying above Murino's head, and then began his own run from the captain.

The captain ran down a sloping path and saw the two figures meeting and running toward a car parked in the shade of a large pine tree. Murino stopped and watched as they jumped into the car, made a sharp U-turn, and headed down the road away from the vineyard. He didn't get a look at their faces, but he was certain he had confronted one shooter by the Banco di Napoli ATM.

Murino put his weapon back into the waist of his jeans and drew a deep breath. It had been years since he had been in this kind of action, and he could feel the adrenaline rush he experienced slowly ebbing from his system. He leaned against a stone wall and stared down at the bay, at the view he so cherished, his calm now ruined by the rain of bullets.

He wiped the sweat off his brow and closed his eyes. He knew from experience that most gun battles are shoot-and-miss affairs, so different from what is seen in movies and television shows. He thought back to what he was once told by an instructor at the Academy, that the accuracy rate of the best police marksman is 16 percent. The number scales a bit higher for a professional assassin. And on this early evening, Murino was thankful the two shooters who had come at him were nowhere near that skill level.

Yet he had one nagging doubt. They were both close enough to potentially have landed one, if not two of their rounds. He was shooting in the blind, but they were shooting at a still target. Was it nerves that caused them to miss their mark? Or was this first attempt nothing more than a warning, letting him know they were studying his routine and could get to him any time they so desired?

There was one other possible explanation. The men were hired as decoys and their sole function was to make Murino believe they were the contracted shooters. If this were the case, then it would allow the actual shooter to make his move when it best suited him and when Murino would least expect it.

And even more dangerous to consider was the possibility that if the men were indeed decoys, then the man assigned to take him down was someone already in place on the island.

Someone who didn't need to learn Murino's habits and comings and goings. Someone who had studied him for weeks, if not months. Someone close enough to know all he needed to know about the captain.

Someone who would not miss when the moment arrived.

31.

CAPTAIN MURINO, IN full carabinieri uniform, walked down the center aisle of the main floor of one of the most notorious of the two hundred and six prisons in Italy. He was escorted by two corrections officers through the intricate passages, watching and waiting as they opened a series of large prison gates and led him around through the mazelike corridors. The prison smelled of a mix of disinfectant and dried urine. The thick walls were painted in off-white colors, a strange mix of gray and yellow. The air was steamy and stifling, making Murino feel as if he were wrapped in soiled woolen blankets. He waited as one of the officers opened a prison gate, this one smaller than the previous ones they had passed through. He followed the two officers in and walked with them along a tight hallway, two thick green iron doors with glass mesh wire squares in the center on either side, and a third at the rear of the hall. The two guards stopped at the last door.

"He's waiting in here," one of them said. His tone was harsh, his words spoken in a thick Milanese accent. "Once you're in, we lock you in. When you're through, bang on the door and we'll let you out. We'll be waiting here."

"Be careful," the second guard said in a gentler tone. "You're not armed. But I can't swear to it he's not."

"Didn't you search him before bringing him to the room?" Murino asked.

"Twice," the guard said. "And we think he's clean. But you would be surprised how many ways these prisoners can hide a weapon on their body. No matter how many times and in how many ways we check them."

"I wouldn't worry," the other guard said to Murino. "When he heard he had a visitor today, he didn't react much. But when he was told it was you, he couldn't wait until you got here. He seems eager to talk to you. I gather you two have a history."

Murino looked at the guard and took two steps back to give him room to open the thick green iron door. After a loud snap, the guard gave the door a slight push and stepped aside and let Murino pass.

He stood in front of the door for a moment as it was locked behind him. He stared across the room furnished with two wooden chairs, both chained and bolted to the floor, and a small ceramic table, its legs wedged and sealed into four small openings in the concrete base.

There was one other man in the room, standing with his back against the cold gray wall. He had his arms folded across his chest and one foot crossed over the other. He had aged since Murino had last seen him, his hair grayer now and thinner. His body was still workout solid, and his eyes were those of a ghost, threatening and filled with evil intent. He was wearing prison-issued green T-shirt and loose-fitting black sweatpants, white socks, and sandals. Multiple prison tattoos were visible on his arms and neckline.

Murino walked deeper into the room and stood by the bolted chair closest to him. "Mind if I sit?" he asked.

"A chair is all I can offer you," the man said, not moving from the wall. "I would have liked to put out a nice platter of antipasti, some mineral water, and a Super Tuscan. But, as you can see, I'm limited in what I can do."

It had been a bit more than eight years since Murino had laid eyes on the man he'd helped place behind the bars of this very prison. It was a warm spring morning, back then, as he sat in a packed courtroom and stared up and listened as an elderly judge handed down a twenty-six-year prison sentence on Guido Ostino, the notorious boss of the syndicate he had worked so hard to bring to ruin.

"You've come a long way to see me, old friend," Ostino said to Murino. "Not that I'm complaining. The more years that pass, the fewer visitors I get. It's easy to be forgotten when you've been out of sight as long as I have."

"I checked the visitor logs before I came in here," Murino said. "You haven't been as lonely as you pretend. You still have a fair number of friends who stop by. Some, I imagine, to reminisce, others to pass on information, a few to sneak in some contraband items, and then those very special few who come to do your bidding."

Ostino curled his upper lip into a half smile, half snarl. "My bidding, as you refer to it, doesn't extend beyond asking for a second shower during the week and maybe a glass of sparkling water to drink on Sunday instead of this swill not even a sewer rat would drink," he said. "Aside from that, I have no greater powers. You made sure of that years ago."

"You had enough power to pull off a riot three summers back," Murino said. "Or so I was told."

"That wasn't a riot, Captain," Ostino said. "That was a protest. One lodged by the prisoners against government restrictions on our health care, which, as it currently exists, is minimal at best."

"Not exactly a peaceful protest," Murino said. "Cells were set on fire, convicts took to the rooftop and tossed heavy items off, injuring several people. Some required medical attention, and a few had to be hospitalized."

Ostino shrugged and stepped away from the wall. He sat down across from Murino and rested his arms on the small table. "You use what there is to use," he said. "The point was made, that's all that mattered."

"A judicial magistrate made a point as well," Murino said. "He had ten additional years tacked on to your prison sentence."

"They had to blame someone, and who better to blame than me," Ostino said. "I've had a target on my back since you were a carabinieri cadet. I've grown used to it. To me, it's a badge of honor. But now I hear rumblings that there's a target on your back. Must be a strange new feeling for you. Let me ask you, Captain, can you get as used to it as I have?"

"Probably not," Murino said. "But that target won't be on my back for very long."

Ostino smiled. "You've changed since we last butted heads," he said. "The years on that island have made you soft, taken away your edge. I can hear it in your voice. The guy sitting across from me now would never have been able to take me and my crew down. You've found love on that island, and in your business, just like mine, that's a weakness."

"The thought has crossed my mind as well," Murino said. "I have changed. *Mellowed* might be a better word. And I have found love on Ischia, both a fiancée who one day will be my wife and the mother of my children and an old widow I have come to think of as a mother. And those two women are the main reasons I came to visit you today."

"You see, Captain, what you just said proves my point," Ostino said. "Those two women, your future wife and the old widow, they are points of weakness. And that will make any target on your back, either from me or from some other enemy you made in your years in the North, that much bigger. You see, you don't need to be the one brought down. Losing your fiancée and this old widow will do you more damage than a bullet to the heart. You might still be breathing, still be a captain in the carabinieri, but your life will be over. It will be as if you are buried next to the ones you love the most."

"I will do everything within my power to see that that never happens," Murino said. "But in the event the men you've sent to Ischia bring about such a tragedy, then you are right, my life will be over. Which will make it meaningless. Just as yours is at this very moment."

"It may not be as meaningless as you seem to think," Ostino said. "Otherwise, why would you drag yourself all the way up here to see me? You may have led the team that brought an end to my crew and put me inside this cage. But you are not free of me yet, Captain. Our fight continues. Me in here, you back in Ischia. If it ends my way, the guilt will belong to you alone. And the blame will rest heavy on your shoulders."

"Maybe so," Captain Murino said, standing. "You think yourself safe behind these walls. A former boss with your feared reputation. You are to be respected. No one would dare touch you. You sleep at night finding comfort in that belief."

"I'm as much a hero on the inside as you are on the outside," Ostino said. "That's a fact of our chosen way of life."

"But just as I have enemies out on the streets of the cities I've worked in, I also have managed to make a few friends," Murino said. "Some of them confined to this very prison. It doesn't take much to turn a criminal from an enemy to a friend. Sometimes all it takes is a talk with a seasoned prosecutor, asking him to cut a ten-year term to a three-to-five in return for some information of value from the defendant. Or sometimes asking a medical friend to help a sick child of a man serving time for a robbery. Or, better still, just waiting it out until a fellow inmate whose brother, cousin, friend your crew left to die finds the courage to come after the man that put them in that cold grave."

"In that case, Captain Murino," Ostino said, "one of us will end up the winner and the other the loser. As always, time will be the final judge."

"You have already lost, Ostino," Murino said, glaring down at the sitting crime boss. "You just don't know it yet. That's really what I came up here to tell you. You will lose your fight and you will die within these walls. Your time is over. I started the job in Florence, and I will finish it back in Ischia. On that you have my word."

32.

THE PIRATE EASED the motorboat gently into the mouth of the cave. He killed the engine and let the boat drift against one side of the gray rocks. He turned and tossed a thick rope to the Magician. "Tie her off around one of the bigger rocks," he said. The Magician stood on the wooden gunwale of the motorboat, wrapped the rope around his upper arm, and tossed it against the rocks. Then he stepped off the boat, searched for the largest rock, and easily tied the rope around it, securing it with a sailor's knot.

The Pirate turned to Nonna Maria, sitting with her back against a blue cushion, large black tote bag resting between her feet. "I'll get out first," he said to her. "Then I'll help you out. You might want to leave that tote bag in the boat again. It's going to be tight in there, and I have enough gear to carry as is."

"Not this time," Nonna Maria said. "This time the bag comes with me. And we might need what's in there as much as we'll need the rest of the things you'll be carrying."

The Magician stood before the entrance to the cave and looked down at the words scrawled in white across the opening. He turned back to Nonna Maria and the Pirate and smiled. "I can't believe it," he said. "It's lasted all these years, despite the humid air and cold water."

Nonna Maria took the Pirate's hand, stepped onto the rocks, and looked down at the three words—THE MAGICIAN'S CAVE. "You had your own cave?" Nonna Maria said.

"It was written a long time ago," the Magician said. "I was young and a bit full of myself. I thought knowing that it belonged to me would keep other smugglers away from it."

"Instead, it drew them in like flies on a hot summer day," the Pirate said. "In little time, this became the one cave everyone wanted to use. If it was safe enough for the Magician, it would be safe enough for everyone."

"It worked in the competition's favor at first," the Magician said. "Then we got a little wiser and started writing it on a few other cave entrances, and in those we set traps. Soon enough, anything that had my name on it, no one went near."

"Are you sure this isn't one of the ones with the traps?" Nonna Maria asked.

"There's only one way to find out," the Magician said, bending his head and stepping into the cave entrance.

The Pirate stood next to Nonna Maria. He had a large backpack on his bare shoulders and a thick coil of rope around each arm. Around his waist he had on a thick belt, a sword, a flashlight, and a set of flares slotted in each of several openings. He looked at Nonna Maria holding the heavy black tote bag. "You sure you don't want to leave that in the boat?" he asked. "I'm loaded down, and the Magician needs his hands free to check for any traps we might come across."

"I gave birth to seven children," Nonna Maria said. "If I could carry each one around for nine months, I can carry a tote bag around for a few hours."

"By now I should know it is a waste of words to try to talk

you out of doing anything you don't want to do," the Pirate said with a smile.

"With age comes wisdom," Nonna Maria said.

She lifted the tote to her shoulder and lowered her head and entered the cave.

They turned three corners before they lost the light. The Pirate pulled out his flashlight and shone it around the darkened cave. The Magician took the folded map from his shirt pocket, opened it, and handed it to the Pirate. "Shine a light on it," he said. "There's an arrow drawn in ink pointing left and next to it a faded drawing of what looks to be an elephant's tusk. Like the one on the wall in front of us. Do you see it?"

"Yes," the Pirate said. "But the wall it's pointing to is sealed."

"I know," the Magician said. "I'm the one who sealed it, and if I haven't lost my touch, I'm the one who can open it."

Nonna Maria rested her tote bag on a dry rock and looked at the path to her right. "Do you hear that?" she asked. "Those sounds?"

The Magician held his ground. The Pirate turned off the flashlight. "If we're lucky, it's the rats scurrying away from the noise we're making," the Pirate said.

"Rats would move away from noise," Nonna Maria said. "These sounds are coming closer."

"She's right," the Magician said. "We're not alone. We have company."

"What do we do?" Nonna Maria asked.

"The only thing there is to do," the Magician said. "We hide."

33.

THEY STOOD WITH their backs against a cold rock wall, hidden in darkness, their faces, arms, and legs coated with the cold moisture streaming down the sides of the boulders surrounding them. The voices were closer now. Three, maybe four men carrying torches were easing their way around the curves of the cave. They had come in from a different entrance and were now only a few feet away from them.

"We're hidden too deep inside this crevice for them to see us," the Pirate said. "Even with their torches."

"Wait until they pass us," the Magician whispered to Nonna Maria. "Once they do, raise your hand, place your fingers against that stone next to your ear, and press it. You don't need to press it hard. Just a little push will do the trick."

"What's the trick?" Nonna Maria whispered back.

"What kind of a magician would I be if I told you?" he said.

"I don't know," Nonna Maria said. "You're the only one I've ever met."

The four men walked past them, their torches pointing forward, inching their way around the curve of the cave, their free hands pressed against the sides of the walls. They were all young and speaking in a language Nonna Maria had never heard.

"Pirates," the Pirate whispered.

"Real pirates," Nonna Maria whispered back, smiling at him.

The Magician waited until the four had made their way around the next bend. "Press the stone now, Nonna Maria," he said.

Just as Nonna Maria reached out a hand to place two fingers on the small stone above her right ear, she felt a hard object pressed against her side. The Magician and the Pirate looked over her shoulder, and their look told Nonna Maria all she needed to know.

There was a fifth pirate in the group.

He grabbed Nonna Maria and pushed her away from the wall, aiming his weapon now at the Magician and the Pirate. He then shouted in the direction of the other four pirates, and soon they stood bunched together in the narrow pathway, their torches held high, eyeing them with a bemused expression. One of the pirates stepped forward, handed his torch to the youngest of the group, and stepped closer to the Magician. He pulled a cigarette and a toss-away lighter from his pocket, lit the cigarette, and drew in a deep drag. "We're all searching for the same thing," he said, now speaking in fluent Italian. "You can make it easy by telling us where it is."

"If we knew where it was," the Magician said, "we wouldn't be standing here talking to you."

"But you must know how to find it," the man said. "Why else would you be down here?"

"We would be more than happy to help you," the Pirate said, "if we knew what it is you think we're looking for."

The man tossed his cigarette to the wet cave floor and smiled at the Pirate. He then turned his attention to the Magician and held his gaze for a moment. He was tall and lean, with sun-blasted skin and eyes that glowed in the shadow of the torches. "We followed you around some of the bends and curves of the cave," he said. "You seem to know your way around. There was very little guessing on your part. On our own, I wouldn't know which way to turn. And I've heard enough stories about these caves that none of us want to spend the rest of our days living in the dark. So that means you either know, or you have something that tells you which way to go."

"You're not from this island," the Pirate said. "But we are. That makes a big difference. We've been inside these caves since we were children. But you're right about one thing. One wrong turn and the rats will find you before anyone else."

The man turned to Nonna Maria and glanced down at her black tote bag. "What's in the bag, old woman?" he asked.

"Food, wine, and water," Nonna Maria said. "Coffee, too."

The man smiled, exposing a lower row of gold teeth. "This seems a strange place for a picnic," he said. "Don't you think?"

"Not if you like to eat in the shade instead of under a hot sun," Nonna Maria said. "But I'm the wrong one to ask. I only eat in my kitchen."

The man nodded and turned back to the Magician. "We've heard rumors of a treasure map," he said. "And I figure if anyone would have it, you'd be the one. So, if you hand over the map, we'll be on our way. You'll be free to go."

The Magician looked at the Pirate, nodded, and smiled. "I'll play along," he said. "Let's say there is a map and I have it and hand it over to you. You think that's all you'll need to get you through these caves?"

"With a map, I'll take my chances," the man said. "It will

give us a head start on anyone else out there looking for the treasure and slow you down at the same time."

The Magician looked at Nonna Maria and then reached into a front pocket of his cargo shorts and pulled out the map given to Rita by her grandfather. He handed it to the man. As the man unfolded the paper and studied the map, the Magician reached out a hand and gently eased Nonna Maria closer to him, placing her with her back against the cold, wet stone wall. "I don't want you to melt from the heat of those torches," he said to her. "Rest yourself against the rocks, and if you need to steady yourself, use your left hand."

"You got your map," the Pirate said to the man. "That puts you one step ahead of us and anyone else that might come looking. But be aware. Map or not, we're going to keep searching for the treasure."

The man looked at the Pirate, refolded the map, and placed it in the rear pocket of his brown shorts. "I wish you luck," he said. "But without a map, the three of you are working off memory, and that's no way to look for any treasure. Especially when you're dragging an old lady along with you."

"An old lady with food and drink," Nonna Maria said.

The man shook his head, turned, and signaled his four companions to start moving around the next turn in the cave. As the last of the group rounded the curve, the Magician nodded to Nonna Maria. "Press the stone now," he said.

Within seconds, the ground at her feet shook and she heard a trembling noise above her and to her right. A large chunk of wall had slid from one end of the cave to the other, sealing the five men inside the passageway.

Nonna Maria and her friends eased themselves out of their

hiding spot, wiping at the dampness around their eyes with the back of their wet hands. Nonna Maria reached into her tote bag and pulled out three folded cloth napkins. She handed one to the Magician and one to the Pirate and kept one for herself. They dried themselves as best they could, the cloth napkins soaked within a span of seconds. "How long before they get out of the cave?" she asked the Magician.

"A few hours if they're lucky," he said. "By morning if they're not. They'll eventually find the opening that will lead them out toward the bay."

"I don't know if there's any lost treasure down here," the Pirate said. "But for pirates to show up this soon after Paolino's death, and with other treasure hunters sure to follow, that tells me there are plenty out there who believe there is."

"Yes," the Magician said, nodding. "And if we're going to be the ones to find it, then we're going to have to move much quicker than anticipated."

"And we need to do it without Paolino's map," Nonna Maria said.

"Don't worry about the map," the Magician said. "I've studied it long enough to draw it from memory. I wouldn't have given it up otherwise."

"We're going to need more than a map to find what needs finding," the Pirate said. "Which means we need a better plan."

"We need to stop thinking as though we're running contraband wine and cigarettes," the Magician said. "We need to think the way Paolino did. We need to think like a jewel thief."

"That sounds like something that would be better done on a full stomach than an empty one," Nonna Maria said.

She reached into her tote bag and pulled out two large panini, one for the Magician and one for the Pirate. "One's eggplant parmigiana, the other is breaded chicken cutlet with roasted peppers," she said. "You decide between yourselves which you prefer. You can eat them while we walk back to the boat."

"I'm so happy I didn't talk you out of bringing that black tote bag along," the Pirate said, choosing the eggplant parmigiana.

"You'll be even happier to know that I packed two bottles of D'Ambra white wine," she said.

"I'm starting to think you're the real magician on this team, Nonna Maria," the Magician said, biting into the breaded chicken cutlet. "I was worried about you coming out on the boat with us and into the caves. And worried when the pirates surrounded us. But you handled yourself well. Now I'm starting to think the Pirate was right. There isn't anything you can't do once you put your mind to it."

"There is one thing I can't do," Nonna Maria said, inching her way around a corner of the cave, the weight of her tote bag now much more manageable. "Never have, and it's too late for me to learn."

"What would that be?" the Magician asked.

"I can't swim," Nonna Maria said.

34.

ALDO AND LUIGI sat at a corner table of the quiet restaurant facing the mouth of the port. They were growing restless and impatient with Carnale, and with the job as a whole. If they had been put in charge of the task, they would have done more than shoot a few stray bullets at the carabinieri captain in the vineyard. They would have made sure he was dead. "I don't know what's holding him back," Luigi said. "If he has a plan, it would be nice to share it with us."

"Only Carnale knows the details of the job," Aldo said. "We think it's to take out the carabinieri captain. But maybe we weren't the ones given that assignment. Maybe we're supposed to give the carabinieri the idea we were sent here to kill him."

"Maybe, maybe not," Luigi said. "Either way, if a move isn't made in the next day, two at the most, I'm walking away."

"And go back and tell the boss what?" Aldo said. "That we got tired of waiting? They want this carabinieri captain taken out, and the boss picked either Carnale or someone we don't know to do the job."

Luigi was trying to catch a passing waiter's attention when he spotted the two women dressed in black. They sat at a table next to them, rosary beads curled around their hands, heads bowed, the words of their prayers spoken in whispered tones.

"What do you suppose that's all about?" Luigi asked, tilting his head toward the two women.

"Some people pray before they eat," Aldo said with a shrug. "Either that, or the food in this place isn't worth the price."

They turned when they saw a motorboat quietly glide into an open slip in the dock, directly opposite where they were sitting. In the boat were two other women, also dressed in black, sitting and staring at both men in silence.

"What's going on tonight?' Luigi asked. "These two at the table. The two on the boat. All dressed in black. Is it supposed to have some meaning, you think?"

"It means it's time for you to leave the island," Cesare Monte said. He stood at the side of the table, his massive body relaxed, staring down at both men. The two men sat frozen in fear. "The two women in the motorboat will take you to Molo Beverello. There will be a car waiting for you there."

"To take us where?" Aldo asked, his mouth dry, sweat coursing down his back and along the sides of his neck.

Cesare Monte glared at the two men. "To where I tell them to take you," he said, his voice low, his manner calm. "You'll be in a city you don't know well. A city you shouldn't have come to in the first place. My city."

"We didn't mean any disrespect when we took the job," Luigi said. "I swear to you, we believed your permission had been granted. We would never have come here otherwise."

"Did you ask?" Monte said.

"We're not in any position to ask," Aldo said. "We get told what to do and where to go. No questions asked."

"But once you got to Naples, you could have come and asked," Monte said. "It would have saved you a great deal of time and trouble. Since whoever you asked would have told you not to bother coming to Ischia. They could have told you to turn around and make your way back to the North. That would have been the smart move."

"If we had done that, we would have been in trouble with the boss who sent us," Luigi said. "And here we are in trouble with you. There doesn't seem a right move to make. Not for us."

"There's only one move left to you now," Monte said. "Get in the boat with the Mourners and have them take you to Naples."

"We know what will happen once we're in Naples," Aldo said. "We've been in this life long enough to know what you will do to us."

Cesare Monte pulled a chair from a free table and placed it next to Luigi and Aldo and sat down. He rested his hands on the table and looked from one man to the other. "The boat with the Mourners gives you a chance to get out of this alive," he said. "Your only chance."

Luigi and Aldo remained quiet for several moments, letting the full weight of Cesare Monte's words settle. "We don't work for you," Luigi said. "We're not your men. How do we know that once we're in Naples, we'll be free to make our way back to the North?"

"You don't," Monte said. "That's the risk you're taking. But then, what is a life without a little bit of risk? But I will tell you this: By leaving now, you might end up on the lucky side of this situation."

"How?" Luigi asked.

"If a carabinieri captain dies in the shadow of a city I control, that will bring the law close to my door," Monte said. "That's not something that would please me. If that were to happen, I would go looking for someone to blame. And I would spare no one."

Cesare Monte pushed back his chair, stood, stared down at Luigi and Aldo, then turned and walked away, disappearing into the silence of the night. The only sounds that could be heard were the lapping of the waves against the docked boats along the port and the low murmurs of the two Mourners still deep in prayer.

35.

IT WAS A cloudless summer morning. Nonna Maria and Captain Murino were in Lacco Ameno, standing along the port side, within sight of the large volcanic mushroom, long a tourist attraction, jutting out from the bay. They ignored the crowded shops and restaurants that were crammed along the boulevard across the way, their attention focused on the sun-drenched sea and the serenity of the horizon.

"It's so peaceful and beautiful," Captain Murino said. "And quiet. I have learned never to take these moments for granted."

"My father used to take me here when I was a child," Nonna Maria said. "We would come on a cart pulled by a mule, down from the port. My mother would pack a lunch for us, and we would sit by the edge of the dock and eat together, and I would listen to the many stories he shared with me."

"What sort of stories would he tell you?" Captain Murino asked.

"He always began with the prison cells," Nonna Maria said. "The ones out there in the middle of the bay. This time of day, you can just see the tops of them."

Captain Murino peered out and searched out the prison cells on the horizon and pointed when he finally caught a glimpse of them. "I've never noticed them before," he said. "Why are they out there?"

"They were used centuries ago," Nonna Maria said. "They would emerge at low tide and prisoners would be taken out there by boat and locked inside the three large cells."

"Left to burn under the heat of a scalding sun," the captain said. "And when the tide came in?"

"The cells would sink into the waters of the bay," Nonna Maria said, "and the prisoners would be left to drown. My father would tell me that the streets would be crowded with people standing along the dock, watching, waiting, and cheering for men to die a horrible death. Their hands were bound, and their mouths filled with straw. No one would hear them scream. No one would hear their cries. They would be swallowed up by the water and disappear."

"Why do you think your father would bring you here and tell you such a story?" the captain asked.

"My father had seen the worst of life," Nonna Maria said. "He was a prisoner himself, during the war, for seven years, under both the Germans and the British. In a prison in North Africa."

"A POW," Captain Murino said.

Nonna Maria nodded. "Those years changed him in many ways," she said. "It was important for him to let his children know, daughters as well as sons, that we would each face our own dark moments. And that we needed to be ready for when those moments arrived and not to be afraid. Never to be afraid."

"Your father taught you well, Nonna Maria," the captain said. "Since I've been here in Ischia, I've never known you to be afraid of anything or anyone."

Nonna Maria smiled. "I've learned to hide it," she said. "The older I get, the better I am at hiding it."

"I believe that's true," Captain Murino said. "When I was a young carabiniere, I would take on any assignment, no matter how dangerous, and never once did I go into those assignments feeling any fear. But now, knowing the dangers I soon must confront, I can almost taste the fear."

"That's because you have so much more to lose now," Nonna Maria said. "A woman you love and who loves you in return, living here, on an island where you both can make a home and build a family. Anyone would be afraid to lose that."

"I also have a great friend," the captain said. "A friend who I would never want to lose."

Nonna Maria looked over at him and smiled. "That's something we have no control over, Captain," she said. "We all lose the ones we love, sometimes too soon. That was always my biggest fear, losing my Gabriel or one of my children. But when he got the disease no doctor can cure, I wasn't afraid. I was ready for the dark moment when it arrived at my door. And I stayed that way, up until he took his final breath. For all those months, I did everything I could to keep the fear away, the fear of living without him."

"You mourned him then," Captain Murino said. "And you still mourn him all these years later, wearing the widow's black. It's a custom that isn't kept much anymore these days."

"After the funeral, and after everyone had left and I was alone in my home, our home, for the very first time, that's when I faced that fear, that fear I had kept hidden away for so many months," Nonna Maria said. "I screamed into a towel, a silent scream no one heard, like those prisoners drowning out in those cells so long ago. I screamed for the longest time, fighting against that fear."

"I haven't had a full life with Loretta as you did with Gabriel," Captain Murino said, "but if I were to lose her, I don't think I would ever recover. I think there's no coming back from such a heavy loss."

"Well, Captain," Nonna Maria said, "then let's both work to make sure that that doesn't happen. These men who have come here to do you harm, they must be defeated. They have left you no other choice. And you don't have to go back and be the man you once were in Florence to beat them. You will beat them as you are now."

Captain Murino rested a hand on Nonna Maria's arm. "There were four men sent here from the North," he said. "My men tell me that two of them left the island for Naples late in the night. A Coast Guard cutter saw two men matching their description in a motorboat driven by two women dressed in widow's black. I wouldn't be taking too big a leap if I were to think those two women were friends of yours."

"I have many friends, Captain, as you by now know," Nonna Maria said. "A few of them are widows, same as me. And a few of them have motorboats."

"And how many of these widows with motorboats that you know would take two strangers on a late-night ride to Naples?" Captain Murino asked, not bothering to hide his smile. "Leave them at the dock and then make the journey back to Ischia, under a starlit sky?"

"Maybe they were doing it as a favor," Nonna Maria said. "From one friend to another."

36.

PEPE THE PAINTER sat across from Nonna Maria. They ignored the heavy foot traffic around them, locals and visitors alike enjoying a late-night walk. They were at Pepe's normal workstation, in front of the Villa Angela, on Corso Vittoria Colonna. Pepe's artwork was spread out behind him and along the walls of the Villa, but his attention was focused on the large portfolio filled with sketches and notes resting on his legs.

"I can't believe it, Nonna Maria," Pepe said, his voice filled with emotion and energy, his brow wet with sweat. "It was in front of me all this time. I was just looking in the wrong places. But finally, I believe I've found the missing pieces we need."

"Good thing, then, that I brought something for you to eat and drink," Nonna Maria said. "A bottle of white wine, two bottles of mineral water, and your favorite, linguini in a white clam sauce, with a few hot cherry peppers mixed in to give it a little more flavor."

"I'll eat later," Pepe said. "This is much more important."

"It must be," Nonna Maria said, "for you to pass on my clam sauce."

"I went through all my sketches from when I first started painting the castle," Pepe said. "Back in those years, I spent hour after hour, day after day, learning as much as I could about our beloved castle. Its history alone took me months of study to learn. I needed to know as much as I could about it. I wanted my work to reflect the history of the structure and to accurately depict not only what you can see from the outside, but what's hidden inside."

Nonna Maria nodded. "Few know the castle as well as you do," she said. "That's why your paintings sell as well as they do."

"Maybe so," Pepe said. "But I've now been painting the castle for so many years, I no longer take the time to look over my notes and no longer read up on its history. I've grown lazy with old age and have allowed my memory to guide me. But the other day, I went home and dug out all my early drawings and notes. It took a while to find them. I hadn't looked at them in years."

"Tell me what you found, Pepe," Nonna Maria said.

"First, a little history," Pepe said. "The original castle was built in the fifth century B.C., but the one we know and see every day dates to the fifteenth century, designed by Alfonso of Aragon. He lived in the castle during its renovations, along with eighteen hundred locals. And there was no road leading to it as there is today. The only access was by water. The road was built in the seventeen hundreds."

"Will any of this history help us find whatever it was Paolino hid inside the castle?" Nonna Maria asked. "Especially now that we have to get by without the map he gave to Rita?"

"It is all of one piece," Pepe said. "The history of the past will guide us to where we need to go."

"That alone is worth a cool glass of wine," Nonna Maria said. She reached into her tote bag and brought out a glass wrapped in foil and a bottle of D'Ambra wine. She unwrapped the foil, tossed it back into her tote, opened the wine, poured a full glass, and handed it to Pepe.

He drank the wine in two long swallows and rested the glass between his feet. "Now, by 1823, Ischia was under the control of the Spaniards," Pepe said. "They turned the castle into a prison. By all accounts it was a brutal prison, and many of the convicts did not live through the end of their sentence. Their bodies were tossed from the castle into the sea. The Spaniards, as well as the locals who lived in the castle, were able to move in and out regardless of the time of day without being seen by any of the convicts."

"How?"

"Alfonso had designed a series of tunnels and passageways that take you from the very top of the castle down to the very bottom," Pepe said. "I have some sketches that will show you exactly what I mean."

Pepe sifted through the papers resting on his knees and handed one to Nonna Maria. "See," he said, pointing the way with an index finger. "It's like a giant maze, one hall leading to another, connected by stairwells giving access to the floors above and below. He designed it as a city within a city."

"And you think these stairs and halls are still there?" Nonna Maria asked.

"I know they are, Nonna Maria," Pepe said. "And I'm not the only one who knew that such passageways existed."

"Who else knew?" Nonna Maria asked.

"That sketch you're holding was a gift given to me many years ago by an old friend," Pepe said. "A friend who studied the castle as much as I did, if not more. For purposes that were much different than mine. He wrote a small note at the bottom of the sketch. Time has worn away at it, smudging it a bit. But the signature under the note remains clear enough for you to read."

Nonna Maria looked down at the sketch, scanning it with the fingers of her right hand. She stopped when she came to the signature, looked up, and smiled at Pepe. "Paolino Iacone," she said.

"You'll also notice that a few of the lines in the sketch match those in the small map that was left to Rita," Pepe said. "This is simply the map on a much larger scale."

"Paolino must have hidden something inside the castle," Nonna Maria said. "He was a man of many talents. And he was also a cautious man, who trusted very few with his secrets."

"And he was devoted to Rita," Pepe said. "She was the only family he had. I don't think he would give her false hopes, especially not on his deathbed. Whatever he left her is inside that castle."

"You've done excellent work, Pepe," Nonna Maria said. "This sketch will be of great help to the Pirate and the Magician."

"There's one more thing you need to know," Pepe the Painter said. "The castle is privately owned today. Has been since 1911, when it was bought by a lawyer practicing here and in Naples. The current owners are still here, living in Ischia. They keep it very quiet, and few know who the real owners are. But you may know them since they carry your maiden name. I would think you must be related by blood somehow. Distant, but blood nonetheless."

"Who?"

"Nonna Maria Mattera," Pepe the Painter said with a wide smile, "the castle is owned by Antonio Mattera and his family."

37.

NICOLA SPAZZI EASED the white carabinieri squad car into an open slot across from the pine gardens near the Bar Calise. He stepped out of the driver's-side door, adjusted his white cap, and slammed the door shut. He leaned against the car and watched Loretta D'Angelo cross the four-way intersection, heading toward the pine gardens.

He moved away from the car and walked in her direction, waving to catch her attention. He nodded at her when she looked his way and slowed her pace as he grew closer. "Is everything all right?" she asked, a touch of tension in her voice. "With Captain Murino?"

"I'm sorry," he said. "I didn't mean to alarm you. Everything's fine with your fiancé. I saw you crossing the street and wanted to see how you were holding up with all these rumors going around."

"I'm fine, Officer Spazzi," Loretta said. "But then I'm not the one whose life is in danger."

"I wouldn't worry about the captain," Spazzi said. "From what I know about him, he can handle any trouble coming his way. He's gone up against much tougher and more dangerous men than the ones that might be sent to Ischia."

"Did you work with the captain when he was stationed in the North?" Loretta asked.

Spazzi shook his head. "I wasn't a member of the carabinieri during that time and was deprived of that honor," he said. "That's the main reason I requested a transfer to be assigned here. To be able to work under his command."

Loretta raised her right hand to shield her eyes from the glare of the sun. She didn't know Nicola Spazzi well, having met him only the few times she had gone to carabinieri headquarters to meet up with Murino. Spazzi seemed too eager to please and always went out of his way to compliment the captain. To her the flattery and attention rang false. Then again, Spazzi might be nothing more than an ambitious young officer, one who held onto the hope that impressing her fiancé would accelerate his own career.

"It was nice seeing you again, Officer Spazzi," Loretta said. "When I see the captain, I'll be sure to mention we ran into each other."

"If you're not in a rush, I was hoping for a brief moment of your time," Spazzi said. "It won't take very long, I promise."

Loretta glanced at the time on her cell phone. "I need to be at work in twenty minutes," she said. "But I like to get there before my shift begins."

"You work a second job in that gift shop across from the newsstand," Spazzi said. "Do I have that right?"

"Yes," she said. "The evenings mostly. When I'm off duty. It's only for the summer season."

"It's not far away," Spazzi said. "I can walk with you if it's not a bother. This way, we can talk, and you will still get to work before your shift begins."

Loretta stayed quiet for a moment and then nodded. They turned away from the entrance to the pine gardens and made their way down the main street, the foot traffic around them not yet as crowded as it would be later in the evening.

"Have you and the captain set a date?" Spazzi asked. "A new one, I mean. I understand an earlier date was postponed."

Loretta glanced at Spazzi and nodded. "We're not quite ready to announce it," she said. "But as soon as we are, I'll make certain the captain makes you aware of the date."

"I don't mean to pry," Spazzi said, raising his hands in mock surrender. "I was just curious. From what I've been able to observe, the locals here tend to marry in the off-season. They also seem to marry other locals. You and the captain are a rare exception."

"You haven't been in Ischia long enough to know the local ways," Loretta said, a low throttle of anger brewing below her calm surface. "I have a cousin who met a young woman from Milan on the Maronti beach. They fell in love and married. They live in Milan most of the year and summer with family on the island. They're about to celebrate their twenty-fifth anniversary."

"Perhaps your cousin was more an exception than the rule," Spazzi said. "I'm guessing he also didn't postpone his original wedding date. Did you know the captain was previously engaged, to a young woman from the North? That wedding was also postponed and, eventually, the engagement broken."

"You seem to want to say something to me, Officer Spazzi," Loretta said, stopping in front of a small church. "It might be better to come right out and say it. Especially since we're close to the gift shop."

"I know we don't know each other well," Spazzi said. "But

you seem like a good person and, in many ways, innocent. I would hate to see you hurt."

"And why would I be hurt?" Loretta asked.

"Take a harder look at Captain Murino," Spazzi said. "He's not the man you like to think he is. There's still time for you to get out before it's too late."

Loretta turned to face Officer Spazzi. "Strong words from a carabinieri officer who claims the only reason he is stationed in Ischia is to work under my fiancé's supervision," she said.

"I wanted to observe his methods," Spazzi said, unfazed by Loretta's anger. "Study his habits and acclimate myself to how he comes to his decisions. I want to know as much about Captain Paolo Murino as I can."

"Why?"

"Why else?" Officer Spazzi said with a smile. "To be as good a carabiniere as I can be."

Loretta looked away from Officer Spazzi and saw Nonna Maria close behind them, her large black tote bag in hand. "Nonna Maria," Loretta said, turning toward her. "What a nice surprise. What brings you out at this hour?"

Nonna Maria smiled at Loretta and cast a glance at Officer Spazzi. "I was at Café Vittoria when I saw you and this young officer talking," she said. "One of my daughters is coming for dinner later and she loves the gelato that Giuliano makes, so I bought a few containers for dessert and for her to take home."

"I don't believe we've met," Officer Spazzi said. "And I may well be the only one on this island who has yet to have that privilege."

"This is Officer Spazzi, Nonna Maria," Loretta said. "He's relatively new to the island."

"It is nice of you to make sure Loretta gets to her job without any problem," Nonna Maria said. "Captain Murino, I'm sure, will be pleased."

Spazzi smiled at Nonna Maria. "Loretta and I were making conversation. Nothing more than that, I assure you."

"You don't need to assure me," Nonna Maria said. "I'm not her fiancé."

"The gelato you purchased could melt buried in that bag you're holding," Spazzi said. "You might want to be on your way before that happens. Besides, an old woman should not be out under this hot sun."

Nonna Maria nodded. "I am an old woman," she said, "but not the only one. Here in Ischia, we're like the pine trees. We're everywhere."

"Then feel free to go on your way," Spazzi said. "And allow me to finish my walk with Loretta to the gift shop."

"Giuliano packed the gelato containers in ice," Nonna Maria said. "He knows I enjoy taking slow walks. Especially under a hot sun."

"And our walk can end here," Loretta said to Spazzi. "I won't mention our conversation to Captain Murino. I'm certain he knows you well enough by now."

"I was going to make a stop at the gift shop," Nonna Maria said. "One of my nephews is working at a bank in Naples and I promised to send him a few bottles of Acqua d'Ischia. He wears it all the time."

"It's our biggest seller," Loretta said, walking past Officer Spazzi and placing a hand under Nonna Maria's right arm. "We can't keep enough of it in stock."

"In that case, we should go before the tourists grab the last remaining bottles," Nonna Maria said.

"Be careful," Officer Spazzi said as Nonna Maria and Loretta began to walk toward the gift shop. "Both of you."

Nonna Maria turned to look at Officer Spazzi. "Old people don't need to be told to be careful," she said. "It's a habit that comes with age."

38.

"I'M NOT SURE exactly what Officer Spazzi wanted from me," Loretta said, standing in front of the display featuring assorted colorful boxes filled with the various scents of Acqua d'Ischia.

Nonna Maria picked up a blue box and then reached for a yellow one. "It was a warning," she said. "Maybe to protect you, but more likely to scare you. And that's not something a carabinieri officer would do or would be sent to do."

"Which tells you what, Nonna Maria?" Loretta asked.

"First, from the words you told me he said, he is no friend of the captain," Nonna Maria said. "Which makes me doubt he asked to be assigned here to learn from the captain."

"Then why ask to come here?"

"That's not a question we can answer with what we know now," Nonna Maria said. "But we do know Officer Spazzi is here on Ischia at the same time as the men who are looking to do him harm."

"You think there's a connection between them?" Loretta asked.

"I would have to believe the worst of Officer Spazzi to think that," Nonna Maria said. "But these men have been here for several days and have made only one move against the captain. And from what the captain told me, not a professional one. The captain is keeping to his normal routine. So why wait? Why take the risk of the captain ordering his men to take them in for any number of reasons? These men have been paid by someone to go after him, but they hold back. Even after two of them were taken off the island, leaving without a word."

"The ones taken by the Mourners," Loretta said with a smile. "At least that's the rumor around the port."

"And we both know better than to listen to rumors," Nonna Maria said, returning the smile.

"In what way would someone like Spazzi be a danger to the captain?" Loretta asked. "While his remarks made me feel uncomfortable, he's still a member of the carabinieri. He might be jealous of Paolo, given his rank and how young he is to be a captain. Could be there isn't more to it than that."

"My eldest daughter, Francesca, loves crime shows," Nonna Maria said. "Watches all of them, and from I've been told, there are plenty to watch. My Francesca has seen more criminals than the most experienced member of any police department."

"I know," Loretta said. "I watch some of them, too. Not as many as Francesca, but enough. I like the British ones better than the American shows we get here, and even better than the ones made in Italy."

"And in all these shows, it's the police who solve the crimes?" Nonna Maria asked.

"Most of them," Loretta said. "A few have private detectives working the cases, and some have civilians helping the police catch a criminal."

"I don't think something like that could really happen," Nonna Maria said, resting four bottles of Acqua d'Ischia on the counter. "Do you?"

Loretta smiled. "Miss Marple is very good at it," she said. "Judging from the few times I've seen her in action."

"She's not a member of the police?" Nonna Maria asked.

"Not at all," Loretta said. "She's an older woman, drinks tea, takes care of her garden, and helps police solve crimes. She's British."

"That wouldn't work in Ischia," Nonna Maria said. "Not many women here drink tea. Now, if you had said wine or espresso, then maybe I would want to know more about this Miss Marple."

"What do the crime shows have to do with Officer Spazzi?" Loretta asked.

"One night while they were having dinner in my home, Francesca and Il Presidente talked about one of the shows they both liked," Nonna Maria said. "And they talked about how they both guessed who the criminal was early in the show. And I was surprised when I heard them say that the one who committed the crime was pretending all along to be a member of the police."

"And that's what you think Spazzi is doing?" Loretta asked. "Pretending to be a carabiniere?"

"No," Nonna Maria said. "Even I know that that would be hard to do. I have no doubt that Officer Spazzi is a member of the carabinieri. Even the old British woman you like would not question that."

"Then what does concern you?"

"Whose side is he really on?" Nonna Maria asked.

She left a twenty-euro bill on the counter, placed the four bottles of Acqua d'Ischia in her black tote bag, lifted it to her shoulder, and turned to walk out of the gift shop. "We'll have our answer soon enough, little one," she said. "A wolf can hide among the sheep only for so long."

39.

EMMITT SHAW BRACED himself against a wet gray boulder, waiting as Barbara Fay made her way up the face of a rock wall toward him, thirty feet above the clear, angry waves splashing against the front of the hard-edged ridge that had stood the test of time for centuries. They were lashed together by ropes, and their iron-toed boots were spiked to give them better leverage against the terrain.

"Twenty feet more and we should be at the opening," Shaw shouted down to her.

"We passed two other cave openings on the climb up," Barbara said as she reached the spot on the rock face where Shaw had paused. "Either one could easily have given us the same access the top one gives us."

"Not if we are in agreement that it would be easier to move the treasure from the top than it would from the bottom," Shaw said. "Cigarettes, whiskey, and other low-end items were stolen in bulk quantities by the contraband smugglers. It made sense to move them from speedboat to the lower caves. Hide them and then move them when the Coast Guard and carabinieri gave up the search."

"The thinking being that if we are looking for something

other than smokes and drinks, that translates to items easily hidden and transported," Barbara said. "And the higher up such valuables are hidden, the less likely that they would be subjected to the harsher elements below."

"Be hard to do much damage to a bottle of Stock 84 packed inside a stout wooden crate," Shaw said. "Or a case of smokes double-wrapped in burlap and sealed in aluminum boxes. But diamonds and jewels are small and can be hidden in anything from a large cask to a thin slot in a wall."

"If that's true, why has every major discovery of stolen treasure always been in deep waters?" Barbara asked. "Buried there not for years, but centuries."

"The ocean floor is nowhere as destructive to fine jewels as the inside of a cave and poses fewer risks," Shaw said. "The lower caves are prone to collapse, burying your fortune behind their walls. The higher up something is hidden, the less likely the risk of a cave-in."

"Only if there is a fortune hidden in these caves," Barbara said. "I know you have convinced yourself, but I have doubts."

"If it turns out you're right," Shaw said, "then the whiskey and the smokes are on me. As well as a fine dinner to go with them."

They struggled upward against the rough terrain, their spikes locking into various small crevices, making it difficult to maneuver. They were also hampered by the heavy gear they were lugging. Shaw had insisted on packing heavy blankets, night equipment, flashlights, flare guns, and enough food to last for three days.

They finally reached the mouth of the open cave. Shaw unhooked his gear and then pulled at the rope, helping Barbara up to the cave. Once they were in, Shaw searched for some scattered plant debris, pulled a few sticks of kindling from his backpack, and tossed it into a pile in the center of the cave soon to be shrouded in darkness. He pulled a butane lighter from a front pocket of his cargo shorts and lit the twigs and straw. Within seconds, he had a fire going.

"Look around for anything you can find that will burn," Shaw told Barbara. "These caves might be cool during the day, but they are as cold as winter at night. The fire will keep us warm and keep the rats from our food supply."

"Rats?" Barbara said with practically a shriek in her voice. "I knew there was something you were keeping from me, Shaw. I don't fear much, but rats are on top of that limited list."

"Not just any old city rats," Shaw said. "These are water rats. Twice the size of anything you'll see on a street in Rome."

"I'm counting on you to keep them at bay," Barbara said.

"I won't let you down," Shaw said. "Now, let's look at those maps and sketches while there's still enough outside light. From here on, it will be crucial for us to know which direction it's best to go."

"What happens if we hear other hunters looking for what we are inside these caves?" Barbara asked.

"You mean like the five pirates that got trapped inside one the other day?" Shaw asked.

"Did that really happen?" Barbara asked.

"The group I overheard talking at dinner last night seemed to believe it," Shaw said.

"Even more reason for us to be prepared," Barbara said. "We need a plan in place in case we hear other hunters coming our way."

"It won't be if we hear, it will be when," Shaw said. "As to whether we follow them or not, it depends on which group it is. If it's a loose band of pirates or some other treasure seekers who know little about the island and these caves, we let them go their own way and gamble they are going down a wrong path."

"And if they're locals?" Barbara asked.

"We deviate for only one local," Shaw said. "The Magician. If we see or hear him, that's who we follow. If there is treasure to be found in these caves, he will lead us to it."

"Until then?" Barbara asked.

"We sit and wait," Shaw said. "Enjoy the beautiful view of the bay. Have our dinner, drink some wine, smoke some cigarettes, if you remembered to pack them, and keep the fire going."

"Sounds exciting," Barbara said.

"We'll read our maps and sketches and plot our path," Shaw said. "That's only a backup plan. We won't really make a move until the Magician figures out the puzzle."

"You seem certain he will," Barbara said.

Shaw shrugged. "I could be wrong," he said. "Many years have passed, his senses might not be what they once were, skills deteriorated. If so, we've wasted time and tossed some money away."

"Or we find what there is to find without him," Barbara said.

"That's possible," Shaw said.

Barbara stared at Shaw for several moments, then shook her head. "You cut a deal with him, didn't you?" she said. "That's why you took on this job. Coming in, you knew you had an inside partner. Someone who would guide you right to the treasure."

"I would not go as far as calling it a deal," Shaw said.

"What would you call it, then?" Barbara asked.

"An arrangement," Shaw said. "An agreement in principle. We are, after all, both in search of the same treasure. I thought rather than compete with one another, we could work together. Especially since no one knows if there's any treasure to be found."

"You trust him?" Barbara asked.

"As much as I trust any treasure hunter," Shaw said. "He's in this for the chase, the same as we are. He's financially set, and far as I know has never burned anyone he went into business with."

"What about the ones he's working with now?" Barbara asked.

"One is his old partner," Shaw said. "Around these parts he's known as the Pirate. The other two are the young girl whose grandfather hid whatever it was he thought worth hiding, and an old widow."

"What's her part in this?" Barbara asked.

"The girl went to her first with the news about her grandfather," Shaw said. "She's not a treasure hunter by any stretch. But she knows everyone on this island, and that can be of benefit to us. Especially if we manage to find something of great value."

"What's the split, assuming we do find a treasure?" Barbara asked.

"The Magician and his crew walk away with fifty percent," Shaw said. "My understanding is they plan on passing all of that to the girl. The other fifty percent comes to us, and we split it as per usual."

"So they're going to all this trouble for free?" Barbara said. "To walk away with nothing?"

"It's a favor," Shaw said. "Nothing more to it than that."

"Do his partners know?" Barbara asked. "That the Magician made a deal with you?"

"That's his decision," Shaw said. "Not mine."

"If the Magician really knows what he's doing, and you wouldn't go into business with him if he didn't, then why are we in a cave, fighting off the cold and the rats?" Barbara asked. "Why aren't we with him, which, wherever it is, I'm certain is warmer and more comfortable than where we're sitting right now?"

"We're here to hold up my end of the bargain," Shaw said.

"Which is what?" Barbara asked.

"To fend off other treasure hunters and pirates," Shaw said. "Protect our partners. Any others who might come looking will think themselves up against two old men, an elderly widow, and a young woman. That is not a confrontation that will give them pause."

"But they won't be expecting us," Barbara said.

Shaw nodded. "We're the surprise guests," Shaw said. "All we need to do is keep the Magician and his small team safe and hope they find something worth finding."

"If they do manage to find something," Barbara said, "will you keep your end of the deal?"

Shaw leaned his head back against the cold, wet stone and stared up at a clear sky crammed with stars and then at the bay below whose swells slapped at the base of the stone foundation. He stayed silent for a moment and then glanced over at Barbara.

"Have I ever?" he asked.

40.

CAPTAIN MURINO SAT across from Nonna Maria, watching her pour two cups of espresso and slide one over to his side of the table. She added three spoonfuls of sugar to hers and with a practiced hand stirred the mixture. "Out of respect for you," Nonna Maria said, "I'll drink my coffee without brandy or chocolate."

"Putting brandy and chocolate in your coffee is not against the law, Nonna Maria," Captain Murino said.

"I'm not worried about breaking any laws," Nonna Maria said. "I'm worried you'll run into my nephew, the doctor, and after he asks how you are, he will ask if you've seen me. Then, knowing my nephew, he will ask if we had coffee together. Since there is no reason for you to lie, you will tell him the truth. And the truth is we did, and I added only sugar, nothing else. You are my . . . what do they call someone who sees someone do something, good or bad?"

"A witness," Captain Murino said. "And in this coffee case, I'm your witness."

"And what better witness than a carabinieri captain," Nonna Maria said.

Captain Murino took a slow sip of the strong coffee and

leaned back in the wooden chair. "I came to see you not just to spend time in your company and enjoy a cup of your delicious, heart-stopping coffee," he said. "I came by for a much more serious reason."

"I know why you're here," Nonna Maria said. "And I don't blame you for being angry. But with all that's going on, I didn't want to put one more concern on your shoulders."

"It always amazes me how you come by your information," Captain Murino said. "I was informed about your involvement in this search for some lost treasure yesterday afternoon. And not even a full day later you knew I would come by and talk to you about it. This, even though I did not mention it to anyone who would mention it to you."

"I heard it from someone who heard it from someone else," Nonna Maria said. "It's the best way for information to be passed on. At least here in Ischia."

"It didn't come to my attention until I received several cables from carabinieri offices in Naples, Milan, and Rome and a phone call from a friend in the Rome Art Squad," Captain Murino said. "They each picked up heavy chatter from various high-level treasure hunters. These hunters, and a few pirates in the mix as well, seem to think there's treasure to be found on Ischia. After a few phone calls of my own, I discover that the one person who holds the key to that treasure is a young woman who came to you for help and advice. And you seem to have given her both."

"There's another reason I didn't bring this to your attention," Nonna Maria said. "We don't know if there is any treasure in the caves to be found. And until I know there is, I don't want to have you waste any of your time."

"Well, these treasure hunters who are coming to Ischia seem

to think otherwise," the captain said. "I don't put much faith in the pirates. They pick up chatter and follow it wherever it leads. Sometimes they get lucky, most times they come up empty."

"We ran into a few the other day," Nonna Maria said.

"You need to tread carefully here, Nonna Maria," the captain said as he finished the last of his espresso.

"I won't walk away from my friends," Nonna Maria said. She rested both hands flat on the wooden table, her empty espresso cup turned over and sitting just beyond her reach. "It is what I do and who I am. If I can help my friends, and that includes you, Captain, then that's what I will do."

"We all love you for that," Captain Murino said. "Every one of us. But there are moments when you need to pull back and let others take the lead. This is one of those moments."

"I've lived long enough to be aware of the risks I sometimes take," Nonna Maria said. "And I know that the things I do make many worry about me. My children, especially my daughters, lose sleep when I involve myself in things they think I should not be involved in. My Gabriel spent many sleepless nights wondering if I would make it back home alive. But he knew me and loved me and understood that what I did was a part of who I am. I'm my mother's daughter, Captain. And, sometimes in simple ways, sometimes dangerous ways, she was always there for a friend in need."

Captain Murino reached out both hands and rested them on top of Nonna Maria's, gazing at her face, their eyes locked. "I would not be able to live with myself if anything happened to you," he said, his voice barely above a whisper. "It would shatter me."

"Then you know exactly how I feel about you," she said.

"So, instead of trying to talk me out of helping you, let's figure out a way to help each other."

Captain Murino stayed silent for a moment, holding on to Nonna Maria's hands, fighting to keep his emotions in check. He then sat back, reached for the espresso pot, and poured himself a second cup. "Where did you hide the chocolate and the brandy?" he said. "I think it's time I drank your espresso the right way."

Nonna Maria pushed her chair back and smiled. "I have fresh pastries in the kitchen," she said. "The ones that go well with a good cup of coffee."

She went into the kitchen and came back with a tray filled with cannoli, éclairs, and babas, a bowl filled with small slivers of dark chocolate, and a bottle of Stock 84. She rested the tray in the center of the table and watched as the captain poured a shot of brandy into his espresso cup and then reached for the bowl filled with chocolate. "How many pieces do I use?" he asked.

"Three will do," Nonna Maria said. "And three spoonfuls of sugar."

Captain Murino dropped three slivers of chocolate into his coffee along with the sugar, stirred, and then took a long swallow. He leaned back in his chair and smiled. "How many of these do you have a day?" he asked, his cheeks flushed.

"Never more than fourteen," Nonna Maria said. "I don't want to make a habit of it."

"I think I'll stay with one for now," Captain Murino said.

Nonna Maria glanced at him and nodded. "Now that you've had your coffee, and before you eat your pastry, let's go over the plan."

Captain Murino shook his head, doing his best to hide the

smile from Nonna Maria. "What makes you think I have a plan?"

"It's something a good friend can always tell," Nonna Maria said.

"It's not so much a plan," Captain Murino said. "For now, let's call it a suggestion."

"One for the treasure and another for the men sent here to kill you?" Nonna Maria asked.

"That's right," Captain Murino said. "Let's take the treasure first. Those on the hunt will have their eyes on you and the friends working with you. How well do your friends know the tunnels and caves on the island? Especially those leading to the castle?"

"No one knows them better," Nonna Maria said. "They can walk them with their eyes closed."

"And the tunnels and caves of the castle lead you to the other ones on the island?" Murino asked. "They're all linked?"

"So I've been told," Nonna Maria said.

"Then have them work from the castle," Captain Murino said. "I'll station men around the perimeter. I'll have them in plain clothes, so as not to attract attention. If my men see anyone who gives them cause for concern, they'll be ordered to bring them in."

"For what crime?" Nonna Maria asked.

"We'll start with suspicious activity," Captain Murino said. "Then, if any of them are armed, we'll tack on a few more charges."

"How about the ones we know are here?" Nonna Maria asked. "How do you plan to deal with them?"

"I'm pretty sure the two remaining men were sent here as decoys," Captain Murino said. "They might take a few runs at me, but they're not here to kill. I fear there's a fifth one out there, someone who has yet to make himself known."

Nonna Maria looked at Captain Murino and stayed silent for a moment. "This fifth one, the unknown," she said. "Is he already in Ischia?"

"I think he's been for quite a while," Captain Murino said. "I have no proof, of course, only intuition."

"Many times, intuition is the strongest proof," Nonna Maria said.

"Intuition is what makes you so good at what you do, Nonna Maria," Captain Murino said. "Back when I worked cases in the North, I relied on my gut instinct to lead me to whoever it was I was chasing. And I was right most of the time."

"You already know who it is," Nonna Maria said.

"I already know who I think it is," Captain Murino responded. "But he needs to show more of his hand before I can be certain."

Nonna Maria leaned closer against the edge of the table. "He's one of yours," she said. "Someone close to you, someone who makes you want to believe you can trust him. That's why you need to be sure."

Captain Murino nodded. "I can't risk being wrong about this one," he said. "I've gone over it so many times in my mind. And all my instincts tell me it's him. But a link in the chain is missing. And I need to find it."

Nonna Maria reached for a small plate, put a cannoli and an éclair on it, and handed it to Captain Murino. "I might know someone who can help with that?" she said.

"Who?" Captain Murino said.

"Who else?" Nonna Maria said. "A friend."

41.

MAURIZIO CARNALE AND Marco sat beside the pool of the Regina Isabella Hotel in the borough of Lacco Ameno, a half-empty bottle of mineral water and two glasses resting on the table between them. Carnale had his head tilted back, overhead sun warming his face and shoulders. Marco sat under the shade of the wide blue umbrella, shifting his feet nervously, his body tense, his words coming out in short bursts. "It's not like them," he said. "Disappearing like that. Without a word to you or to me."

Carnale reached for his water glass and downed half. "They don't matter," he said, placing the glass back on the table. "The job is what's important. And look at the brighter side. With Luigi and Aldo out of the picture, the payday for you and me is now double what it would have been."

"Maybe so," Marco said. "But you listen to some of the talk around the port, and it makes you wonder what we've gotten ourselves into."

Carnale turned to face Marco. "What kind of talk?" he asked.

"I'm not saying what I heard is what actually happened," Marco said. "It might be nothing more to it than rumor and gossip. But it's out there, and while maybe not all of it is true, could be some of it is."

"What did you hear?" Carnale asked, this time with an edge in his voice.

"They left the island late at night," Marco said. "On a motorboat, a couple of women dressed in black taking it out. I overheard some of the guys on the fishing boats mention it. If it's true, why would they do that? Go off-island with two women they probably didn't know?"

"They may be connected to them in some way," Carnale said. "Friends, maybe. Relatives, more likely. Everyone on this island seems connected to one another in some way. Or maybe they got tired of waiting. And for that I don't blame them one single euro."

"No argument from me on that," Marco said. "I thought for sure the shooter would have made his move by now. Especially after what happened up in the vineyard with the captain. If they wanted to, Luigi and Aldo could have taken out the carabiniere and we would have all been home by this time."

"I don't know what's held him back," Carnale said.

"Could be he thinks the captain's on to him," Marco said. "Waiting for the guy to make a false move, lower his guard in some way."

"If that's the case, maybe this guy isn't as good as the bosses think he is," Carnale said. "Maybe he's the one who should have been hired to be the decoy instead of us."

"Maybe we can put a lit match to this guy's tail," Marco said. "Get him to make his move sooner than he planned to."

"Not a bad thought," Carnale said. "We can't take down the carabinieri captain, but nothing is stopping us from going after somebody he's close to."

"The old widow woman, and his girlfriend," Marco said.

"The girlfriend lives at home, and I suspect the captain makes sure she always has eyes on her," Carnale said.

"That leaves the widow," Marco said. "She seems to know everybody who breathes on this island, but she does live alone."

"Not completely," Carnale said. "That guy that told us to back off, Il Presidente, he lives on the first floor of her home. He may not be what he once was, but he's not somebody you can ignore."

"She's the safer choice," Marco said.

"That might be true," Carnale said. "But if Il Presidente thinks the old lady is in any danger, he's not going to need a map and a guide to tell him who put her there. He'll come looking for us. And the carabinieri must follow the law. Not Il Presidente. He has his own set of laws."

"The time comes when we can't handle an old gangster, maybe we shouldn't be in the business we're in," Marco said.

"And what's your idea?" Carnale said. "Use the widow to light a fire under the shooter and force him to make his move against the captain?"

"Unless you got something better in mind," Marco said. "Play around with it for a bit. Look for any booby traps I haven't thought through."

"If this job goes the way it should, the shooter will be the most wanted man in Italy," Carnale said. "The carabinieri won't spend much manpower looking for us, even if we do make a move on the old woman."

"No doubt," Marco said. "The carabinieri won't cut any deals with him. Not for bringing down one of their own. He can give them our names and the names of every member of the crew, it's not going to scratch one single day off his sentence."

Carnale shook his head and smiled. "I'm not worried about what happens to him after he gets arrested," he said. "My concern is what he does before that happens. If the captain goes down, that leaves us. And how do we know part of his plan isn't to take us out too? If he gets you and me out of the picture, he can walk away without any worries."

"You think that's been his plan all along?" Marco asked.

"It's the only plan that makes sense," Carnale said. "He gets rid of the captain and us, there's nobody around to tell the carabinieri how this whole plan shook out."

"What are we going to do to prevent that?" Marco asked. "He can prove we were sent here to take down a carabinieri captain. He'd have no problem on that end. He'd have us right where he wants us."

"Except he's the one who most wants to see the captain go down," Carnale said. "From what I heard, it's a revenge play for him, for what the captain did to the boss he put behind bars."

"We have to handle this the right way," Marco said. "Leave as quietly as we came in. We do that, we get paid, head off the island, hide out for a few months, and wait for another call, from another boss. Get to live and kill another day."

42.

NONNA MARIA SAT on the stone bench in front of Saint Peter's Church. The night was hot and muggy, but despite the excessive heat, Corso Vittoria Colonna was crammed with its usual mix of tourists and locals, all enjoying their early evening stroll. Nonna Maria held a folded white handkerchief in her right hand, wiping at the thin lines of sweat forming on her upper lip. She had always enjoyed sitting and watching the crowd, greeting familiar faces she had known for so long, and admiring the colorful clothing worn by the tourists as they marched past. She always took note how the crowds would grow larger and more diverse with each passing season.

"Would you mind some company?" Cesare Monte asked, standing off to her right, a lit cigar in his left hand. He was dressed in a long-sleeved black shirt, tailored gray slacks, and black Ferragamo loafers. He was holding a small leather bag in his right hand.

"I always make room for a friend," Nonna Maria said.

Cesare Monte smiled and sat next to her. He handed her the small leather bag. "It's from my wine cellar," he said. "I know you prefer the wines of the island, but I thought you would enjoy a taste of Marisa Cuomo wine."

"I like the idea that the wine is made by a woman," Nonna Maria said. "I'll drink it and raise a glass in your name."

"I wanted to bring you something," Monte said. "My mother taught me never to visit anyone with empty hands."

"A wise woman," Nonna Maria said.

"And there's a story that goes with the wine," Monte said. "One I came here to share with you."

"It sounds like a story that should not be overheard by anyone," Nonna Maria said.

"That's probably for the best," Monte said. "Let's walk together, away from the crowd. I find more comfort on quiet streets."

Nonna Maria put the leather bag into her large tote bag, stood, placed her right arm under Cesare Monte's left, and they turned away from Corso Vittoria Colonna, walking slowly down a sloping street along the rear of Saint Peter's Church.

"The story I came to tell you is about a young boy from the North, a troubled boy, his father found dead in an alley, said to be killed by someone to whom he owed money," Monte began. "His mother not able to cope with a strained life, forced to raise three children alone and with very little money and a future that offered little in the way of hope."

"Being poor is a heavy burden," Nonna Maria said. "Like a weight on your back that can never be removed."

"The easy way out is to surrender, and that's what this boy's mother did," Monte said. "She left her children behind and just disappeared. The young boy had two sisters, and he hid from the authorities on the day they came to take them away to a local orphanage. From there he took to the streets, lived on them, and lived off them. He was good at it, good enough that he came to the attention of a crime boss always on the lookout for a talent he could put to good use."

"The boy became a criminal," Nonna Maria said.

"He became what he was meant to become, Nonna Maria," Monte said. "The crime boss took him in, raised him as one of his own, schooled him in the business he knew so well."

"Much as your father did with you," Nonna Maria said.

"My father prepared me to be a boss," Monte said. "The young boy was taught to be an assassin. There's a big difference."

"I know," Nonna Maria said. "I don't have any idea what a boss needs to do to hold his place. And it's not for me to know. But I do remember your grandfather helping my mother through a difficult time and how years ago your father helped me bring a peaceful end to a property dispute. Not to mention how you came to my aid when I came and asked a favor."

"The young boy in my story did not grow to be a man like the ones you know from my family," Monte said. "He was raised to be cold, deceitful, vengeful, to plan his killings with skill and cunning."

"Have you crossed paths with him?" Nonna Maria asked.

"Not yet," Monte said. "But I make a point to know if he ever sets foot in any area under my control."

"And has he?" Nonna Maria asked.

"A number of years ago, the boss who raised him and taught him how to maneuver through the killing fields was caught by the carabinieri and sentenced to a lifetime behind prison bars," Monte said.

He and Nonna Maria stopped by a low stone wall. He helped ease her onto a comfortable spot on the top and stood across from her, his cigar still cupped in his right hand. "Was he arrested too?" Nonna Maria asked.

Monte shook his head. "He was out of the country at the time of the takedown," he said. "When he returned, he swore his revenge against the carabinieri who sent his boss to rot behind iron bars. But he needed time. The carabinieri had wrecked the boss's crew, most of them dead, the ones that weren't sent to prison. So he continued to perfect his craft and hone his skills and waited to make his move."

"For how long?"

"For as long as it took," Monte said. "In his case, several years. Then he had his documents altered, took on a new identity, and joined the enemy. He became a member of the carabinieri, a group he despised more than any other."

"He had to have a good reason," Nonna Maria said.

"The best reason of all," Cesare Monte said. "Revenge."

"And now you believe that man is here," Nonna Maria said. "In Ischia."

"He has been for the past six months," Monte said. "Working out of the carabinieri headquarters. Under the command of your friend, Captain Paolo Murino."

"And he has waited all these years to kill the captain," Nonna Maria said. "Why so long?"

"Anyone can pull a gun and end a life," Monte said. "But it takes a certain kind of dedication to get close to the target, to know his ways, his habits, his likes and dislikes. In some cases, even to become a friend. It takes time to do that and a great deal of patience. And right now, he's in a perfect position to make all that time and effort pay off. That's what makes him such a deadly assassin."

"And all that is worth waiting for so many years to pass?" Nonna Maria asked.

"Patience is part of the skill set of an assassin," Cesare Monte said. "The wait is just as important as the kill. There is a degree of satisfaction that comes from taking out a target after several years have passed."

Nonna Maria stayed silent for several moments and then glanced up at Cesare Monte. "Will you tell me his name?" Nonna Maria asked. "This assassin who is so eager to kill Captain Murino?"

Ceasare Monte nodded. "Spazzi," he said. "His name is Nicola Spazzi. The assassin who has targeted your friend the captain is a carabinieri officer working under his command."

43.

PEPE THE PAINTER had his back to a stone wall, Nonna Maria and Rita standing next to him. They were in the middle tier of the castle, watching as the Pirate and the Magician tied thick coils of rope around their waists and around their arms. Each stood within an arm's length of a large Do Not Enter sign posted in front of the cave entrance to their right.

"It might have been a good idea for the Pirate to put on pants and a shirt," Pepe said. "Or at the very least a pair of climbing boots. The edges of the rocks in the caves and tunnels tend to be sharp. He's bound to come out of there with his share of cuts."

"His skin is as thick as a leather belt," Nonna Maria said. "So is his head. He'll come out the way he went in. Wearing a bathing suit and a bandanna and carrying a sword around his neck. Nothing we say or do will make him change his ways."

"I'll lead them down," Pepe said. "When we reach the first landing, I'll signal you with the flashlight that we made it to the cave. That's when you and Rita move down two flights and wait by the exterior wall on the other side of the cemetery. The one with the Danger High Voltage sign in the center."

"That's the door you want me to go into?" Rita asked.

Pepe the painter nodded. "Yes," he said. "And don't be put

off by the sign. It's only there to keep away tourists and teen-agers."

"Are you sure that that wall opens from the inside?" Nonna Maria asked.

"If the sketches are right, it will," Pepe said. "Paolino used four access walls to move in and out of the caves and tunnels. The only way he could move freely from one to the other without much attention was if they opened from the inside. So, if the first one we try works, then my guess is they all will."

Rita came over and faced them both. "It's time," she said. "The castle closes to visitors in ten minutes."

"Did you remember to pack anything to drink?" Nonna Maria said, reaching down for her black tote bag.

Pepe pointed to the large backpack resting against his leg. "Eight large bottles of water," he said. "That should be more than enough to keep us hydrated."

Nonna Maria pulled out a sweaty bottle of Casa d'Ambra white wine and handed it to Pepe. "Put this in there too," she said. "For the Pirate. He feels the way I do about water."

Pepe looked over at the Pirate and the Magician and smiled. "Whether we manage to find any treasure or not, it's great to see the two of them working together again," he said.

"The money was only a part of it for them," Nonna Maria said. "It allowed them to live the kind of life they wanted. But after a while, they both had more than enough."

"Especially the Pirate," Pepe said. "All he wanted was a motorboat, enough fuel to keep it running, and a few bottles of wine to fill his stomach. And the Magician, from what I understand, invested wisely what money he had, and neither has ever wanted for anything, going on three decades now."

"So why are they helping us?" Rita asked. "My Nonno might not have hidden anything of value in these caves."

"It gives them another chance at what they both most miss," Nonna Maria said. "The chase. They find something in the caves, or they find nothing. It's all the same. The chase is their reward."

The Magician nodded at Pepe as he and the Pirate made their way toward the Do Not Enter sign. "They're ready," Pepe said to Nonna Maria. "You and Rita start heading down. And I don't want you to worry about us. We'll be fine."

"Do you know what you're doing?" Nonna Maria asked.

Pepe the Painter nodded and gave Nonna Maria a gentle pat on the arm. "I do," he said. "And the Magician and the Pirate know even better than I do."

"Then there's no need to worry," Nonna Maria said.

She turned and followed Rita toward the sharp turn leading to the steep steps down to the next level. The setting sun was at their back, and Nonna Maria glanced to her right over the edge of a wall, looking toward Ischia Ponte and the boats gathering in the harbor. "The feast of Saint Anne has always been my favorite," she said to Rita. "Since I was a young girl."

"I think it's because it's the most celebratory of the feasts," Rita said.

"Let's hope that doesn't change after tonight," Nonna Maria said.

44.

CAPTAIN MURINO SPOTTED the motorcycle three car lengths ahead of him, both of them forced to inch forward slowly due to the congested traffic of the port and the throng of pedestrians making their way from the packed hydrofoil to the taxi stand across the way. They were a quarter mile from the open road leading to Cartaromana and the less congested boroughs of the island.

The captain recognized the driver of the motorcycle from the surveillance video taken in front of the Banco di Napoli. It was the younger of the two men, Marco, wearing the same outfit he had on the day they met, and he was riding without a helmet.

As soon as he saw an opening, Marco gunned the motorcycle and made his way up the curving road, free of traffic. The captain maneuvered past an old Fiat and an Alfa Romeo convertible and eased his squad car into a higher gear, fast on the tail of the motorcycle. Marco angled the bike around a sharp curve and then picked up speed, moving past storefronts, fruit vendors, and cafés, running his bike at a speed well past the local limit.

The captain picked up his transmitter and alerted all area police, both local and carabinieri, that he was in pursuit of a speeding motorcycle and needed further assistance. Murino inched his car closer to the rear of Marco's bike and turned on his flashers. Marco turned and glanced at the carabinieri squad car, saw Murino behind the wheel, and swerved from the main road onto a dirt path, near Lacco Ameno. Murino followed in pursuit, both of them leaving behind a thick trail of dust and debris.

Marco spun his motorcycle around a sharp break in the road, taking a 180-degree turn and moving into an area of thick brush. Murino braked to a stop, slammed his car into reverse, and then aimed his car in the direction of the motorcycle. His windshield was thick with dust and shards of grass and twigs, the wipers doing little to clear the captain's line of vision. Murino moved his car through thick hedges and high grass. He couldn't see Marco but could still hear the revving cycle.

Murino followed the sound, moving as fast as he could through the thick brush and along the unpaved road. The sun shone through breaks in the hedges and grass, and a reflection off the front chrome of the motorcycle caused him to glance to his left, where he spotted Marco racing straight toward him, one hand gripping the barrel of a Baretta.

Captain Murino slowed his car, opened the driver's-side door, and unholstered his weapon. He turned the car at an angle and the open door caught the front end of Marco's motorcycle. The bike came to an abrupt stop and skidded into a pile of brush. Marco rolled off the bike, landing with his back to a large pine tree, the gun still in his hand.

The captain killed the engine on his car and stepped out of the vehicle. He walked slowly toward Marco, his gun held low in his right hand. Marco was bleeding from a cut to the side of his head, and his shirt and pants were stained with dust and strips of grass. "This would be a good time for you to toss that gun to the side," Murino said to him.

Marco smiled and shrugged. "And if I don't?" he asked. "What are you going to do then? Shoot me?"

"Yes," Murino said.

"Let's try to remember, you were the one chasing me," Marco said. "I was just going out for a ride."

"Without wearing a helmet," Murino said. "That's a minor offense, but a good place to start. And then you were speeding, and you didn't stop when I asked you to pull over."

"You never asked me to pull over," Marco said.

"I'm aware," the captain said. "But the only ones who know that are the two of us. And I'm guessing I'll be the one that will be believed."

"I could have taken you out anytime I wanted," Marco said. "If it was my call, I'd be talking to a ghost."

"Whose call is it?" Murino asked.

Marco smiled. "If you're waiting for me to tell you that, then you might as well shoot me now," he said. "I'm not going to spoil the surprise."

"Do you know, before I took down Ostino and his crew I made it my business to know everything about him and his operation," the captain said. "And I mean everything—from birth to present day. About everyone connected to Ostino. There aren't any surprises left. It just took a while for me to figure it all out. I'm a little rusty."

"I did wonder why you didn't make a move on either me or Carnale when you first got wind that we were on the island," Marco said. "And why you didn't panic when those other two fools took a few shots at you in the vineyard."

"They were smart enough to leave Ischia when they had the chance," the captain said.

"From what I heard, they really didn't have much choice," Marco said.

"They knew the risks they were taking coming to Ischia," the captain said. "And not just from me."

"So, what happens now?" Marco asked. "Are you going to arrest me?"

"I learned long ago not to waste time on minor charges," the captain said. "Or with minor players. Leave the gun and go find your bike. Head back to the port and look for your friend Carnale."

"And tell him what?" Marco asked. He rose slowly to his feet, leaving the Baretta next to the tree. He dusted himself off and wiped at the blood dripping down the side of his face.

"What I'm telling you," the captain said. "Leave this island now, while you still have the chance to get off it alive."

"And you're the one who's going to take us down?" Marco asked, stepping closer to the captain.

"Only if you're lucky," the captain said.

He stared at Marco for a moment, then turned and walked slowly back to his car and the ride back to carabinieri headquarters.

45.

THE FEAST OF Saint Anne is the most elaborate and spectacular held on the island of Ischia. It is a seaside festival in honor of the mother of Mary, and it opens with a long procession of pregnant women and women who wish to be pregnant, marching from the church in Ischia Ponte toward the mouth of the castle.

The march usually occurs at dusk and is followed by a parade of boats decorated with either humorous or historical displays, decks and masts covered in an assortment of flowers. Prior to the start of the floating parade, dinner is served on the boats, the wine kept in flasks and tied to the outside of the boats, floating in the water, to keep it cool.

"Everyone loves the feast," Nonna Maria's daughter Anna would often tell new arrivals to the island. "It is a celebration for all to enjoy—young, old, and in between. There is something for everyone, starting with the bay of Cartaromana filled stem to stern with boats of different shapes and sizes, competing for the grand prize—the Palio of Saint Anne. For the children, there is the massive fireworks display at the end of the feast, and before that, the burning of the outside of the castle, done in memory of the destruction of the castle centuries ago by the Saracens. Small piles of wood are set ablaze on the edges of the castle walls, to give the impression the castle is under attack. It leaves the locals happy and content, bringing back many memories. And for those new to the island, it makes them realize they are visiting a truly special place."

And for Nonna Maria, it was the perfect night for the Magician, the Pirate, Rita, and Pepe the Painter to search for Paolino's lost treasure.

Nonna Maria walked with Rita down the sloping steps to the next level of the castle, her ever-present black tote bag slung over her right shoulder, holding on to the walls for support as they rounded each curve.

Rita paused and watched Nonna Maria struggle down a steep incline. "We can stop for a few minutes," she said. "It will take them a while to adjust their eyes to the darkness of the caves. So we have time for you to rest."

"The Pirate has eyes like a bat," Nonna Maria said. "And the Magician isn't called that by accident. He can find his way home blindfolded. And they will need those skills to keep up with Pepe the Painter. He moves faster than men half his age. Do not be fooled by the three old men you see. Never forget who they once were. Because they never have."

"Maybe so, Nonna Maria," Rita said, not bothering to hide her concern. "But they haven't been inside those caves and tunnels for more years than they would like to remember. They don't know them as they once did. If they make one wrong turn around a tunnel or walk into the wrong cave, they could be lost to us forever. And no treasure is worth that. I would not be able to live with myself if anything happened to any one of them."

Nonna Maria reached out a hand and rested it on Rita's face. "You have to trust in their skills," she said. "This was once their life, especially the Pirate and the Magician. Pepe explored the caves for reasons of his own, but he knows those caves and tunnels as well as they do, if not better."

"And what if the risks they are taking are all for nothing?" Rita asked. "What if my Nonno gave me an old sketch of a map he had drawn with the promise of a treasure out of some feeling of guilt that he had nothing more than empty words to leave me?"

"Then you have given them the gift of an adventure," Nonna Maria said. "One they will always cherish."

"And what about you, Nonna Maria?" Rita asked.

"My gift is a simple one," Nonna Maria said. "Your grandfather was a friend to me and to my husband. And you came to me for help. I have never looked for any treasure, lost or in plain sight. But I have always done what I could to help my friends. And for me, despite the risks and the chance nothing will come of it, that is all the gift I need."

46.

NONNA MARIA WATCHED Rita ease her way through the partial opening in the wall. She had her back to the large Danger sign, standing across from the entrance to the medieval museum, the steps and walls now shrouded under a blanket of darkness. Below her she could hear the feast underway, music echoing up from all corners, the words and laughter of the mingling crowds easing up the four sides of the castle like vapors, the multitude of boats beginning to fill the bay and surround the stone walls on all sides.

"Be careful," Nonna Maria said to her. "And don't worry about finding them. They will find you and lead you down to the next level. I'll meet you where the Pirate's boat is docked."

"Are you sure you'll be able to make your way down?" Rita said. "It's getting darker by the minute. You won't be able to see where you're going."

"I've been going up and down these corridors since I was a child," Nonna Maria said. "I don't need a light to show me the way. And they'll be lighting the wood on the outside of the castle soon. Even with all the smoke, it will make it bright as a sunny day."

Rita nodded and turned to leave, sliding the stone wall back into place as she did. Nonna Maria turned and began a slow and careful descent down the steps, holding on to the wall. She paused around a bend and pulled a folded white handkerchief from the front pocket of her black blouse and wiped at her forehead and upper lip.

"Old woman like you shouldn't be out in this kind of heat," a male voice from behind her said. "You should be sitting somewhere you can get a bit of a breeze."

Nonna Maria turned and faced Carnale. "At my age the heat is a good thing," she said. "It helps with the aches and pains. A breeze is the last thing I need. It's the fastest way to catch a cold. At least that's what my mother always told me, and she was right most of the time."

Carnale pressed a hand against the small of Nonna Maria's back and pushed her forward. "Let's see if your mother knew what she was talking about," he said. "Go down a few more steps and stay to your right. Stop when you reach the gate that leads to the restaurant."

"I've heard it's an excellent restaurant," Nonna Maria said, moving slowly down the darkened stairwell. "But it would be wasted on me. I eat only in my own kitchen."

"Don't worry," Carnale said. "We're not going there to eat. The place is closed for the night, on account of this big feast going on. Which makes it perfect for us."

"How did you know where to find me?" Nonna Maria asked. "I only mentioned to a few people where I would be, and they're not the kind who would tell a man like you anything about a woman like me."

"That was the easy part," Carnale said. "You've been seen enough times with those three old guys that I figured where they went, you would follow. I don't know what you've got going with them, or with the girl for that matter, but whatever it is, it worked out, because following them led me to you."

"And now that you've found me?" Nonna Maria asked, moving farther down the stairwell, closer to the shuttered gate leading to the five-star restaurant called the Monastery.

"If you stay quiet and do as you're told," Carnale said, "then pretty much nothing will happen. I consider you my protection."

"Protection from what?"

"As long as I have you, neither the carabinieri captain nor your friend in Naples will make a move against me," Carnale said. "You're the fastest and safest way for me and my other friend to get out of here alive."

The wooden scaffolding around the castle was now in full flame, filling the area with thick gray clouds of smoke. The foul air made breathing difficult for Nonna Maria, her lungs feeling the weight of the fumes, her breath coming in and out in short and painful strokes. The noise from the crowd that was gathered along the walkway to the castle and crammed in the side streets of Ischia Ponte had reached its maximum levels, and the harbor was filled with boats of all sizes, decorated in an assortment of colors. Several large statues of Saint Anne floated on wooden rafts among them, draped with strands of flowers and strings of colored lights.

They reached the gate of the Monastery, the iron gate locked, the passageway leading to the restaurant lit by two small overhead lights. Carnale stood next to Nonna Maria, one hand holding her left arm, his back up against the gate, his eyes watering from the thick smoke engulfing them both.

Nonna Maria kept her head down, facing the gate, the fumes making her feel light-headed, the cool air mixing with thick mounds of smoke bringing little relief. Her bad leg ached from the walk, and her legs and arms were coated with a thin sheen of cold sweat.

She lifted her head when she heard the approaching footsteps and saw through the haze a man walking toward them. He was dressed in black, his hands thrust into the pockets of his trousers. He approached the gate, looked for a moment at Nonna Maria, and then turned toward Carnale. "You better know what you're doing with this. We should have done what the captain told us to do. Get off the island."

"Grabbing her buys us some time," Carnale said.

"Time for what?"

"To see if it plays out the way it's supposed to," Carnale said. "We're not just decoys, Marco. That's the part no one told you."

"What else are we?" Marco asked.

"We're the backup team in case the guy given the job doesn't come through," Carnale said. "Then it falls to us."

"A decoy is what I agreed to and it's all I agreed to," Marco said. "It goes the other way and we're both dead. The boss in Naples will not let that stand."

"And the flip side of that is, we can't go back to the North without the job being done," Carnale said. "If the shooter doesn't come through, we need to take out the carabinieri captain."

"However it plays out, we end up under the glare of two bosses—one in the South, the other in the North," Marco said.

"If the shooter is as good as I've been told he is, our worries are cut in half," Carnale said. "Meanwhile, we hold on to the old lady until we see how it all plays out."

Carnale inserted a thick key into the lock and turned it. He took several steps back and swung the gate open, letting Nonna Maria and Marco into the restaurant's courtyard. He then closed the gate and locked it, putting the large key into the front pocket of his black button-down shirt.

"There's a table against the wall," he said to Nonna Maria. "And a comfortable chair next to it. You can sit there while you wait. There's a cold bottle of mineral water and a glass on the table. You're probably thirsty from the walk down the steps and breathing in all that smoke."

Nonna Maria looked at Carnale and tilted her head toward Marco. "I think you should give the bottled water to your friend," she said. "I don't drink water."

"What do you drink?"

"Coffee during the day," Nonna Maria said, "cold white wine by night. But I drink both only in my own house and only with my friends."

"Your choice," Carnale said. "But I'll leave the water there anyway. In case you change your mind."

"It's how I've lived my life," Nonna Maria said. "One night is not going to change it."

"Could be a long wait," Carnale said. "And that smoke out there is only going to get thicker and find its way in here. Then, when the fireworks start, there'll be even more smoke. That bottle of water might start looking good to you by that time."

Nonna Maria walked to the side of a semicircular table and pulled out an iron-backed chair with a thick cushion resting in the center. She sat down and eased the black tote bag off her shoulder and rested it by her leg. She gazed up at Marco and then over at Carnale. "It will have to be a very long wait for me to even think about drinking a glass of water," she said to them.

"If you're tired, there are lounge chairs in the storage room," Carnale said. "We can get one for you. You can lie down and rest while you wait."

"That's right," Marco said. "Rest easy, old woman. If we have you, we'll be safe. No one on this island will risk harming the beloved Nonna Maria."

"It's a gamble," Carnale said. "But it's one we had to make."

"Gamblers always lose," Nonna Maria said. "If you think by taking me, you're protecting yourselves, you're wrong. Someone will come for me."

"The carabinieri captain will have his hands full," Marco said. "He won't have time to look for you."

"I wasn't talking about Captain Murino," Nonna Maria said.

"Who, then?" Carnale said.

"Another friend," Nonna Maria said. "And that's when you will need my help if that friend makes it here."

"And why is that?" Marco asked. "Why would we need your help with this other friend of yours?"

"Because this friend won't come here looking to arrest you," Nonna Maria said.

47.

THE PIRATE TOSSED a rope to the Magician, watching as he caught it with one hand and knotted it around his waist. He then propelled himself deeper into the darkness of the cave. Pepe the Painter and Rita stood on a narrow ledge, their backs against an icy, sharp-edged wall. "How far down will he need to go?" Rita asked.

"About twenty meters, maybe a little less than that," Pepe the Painter said. "As soon as his feet feel soft earth, he'll know to stop."

"Why are you so certain this is the cave Paolino used to hide what he didn't want anyone to find?" Rita asked.

The Pirate looked away from the Magician and turned back to face Rita. "There are hundreds of caves hidden within the rocks and the castle," he said. "But there is only one that's been known since the days of the Moors as the House of Gold. We would have searched for months before we found it. But Pepe's sketches saved us the trouble."

"I first heard about it as a young boy," Pepe said to Rita. "I thought it more legend than fact. But I always wanted to see it, and then, as I got older, to paint it. To bring it to life on a canvas. It has such a great history. It deserves to be preserved."

"And it wasn't just your grandfather who made use of it," the Pirate said. "This cave could well be hiding many fortunes, many lost treasures. From the Greeks to the Romans to the Moors to the pirates who would plunder the seas between here and Sicily and hide their coins and silver within these walls."

"If this is common knowledge, why hasn't anyone come looking for any treasure until now?" Rita asked.

"There are caves such as the ones here in Ischia all over the world," the Pirate said. "Sometimes all it takes is a spark to ignite the fire. Once word got out that there was talk of a lost treasure, the drumbeats began."

"Then word filtered out that there might be a map that would lead to a treasure, and the hunt was on in full swing," Pepe said.

"But I didn't tell anyone except Nonna Maria," Rita said. "And she only mentioned it to the three of you."

"You don't need talk for word to spread," the Pirate said. "It wouldn't have meant much to a treasure hunter if I went looking or Pepe started to move around the caves. But when the Magician surfaced, it didn't take long for other hunters to take notice."

"I found a soft landing," the Magician said from below. "So, if I'm not breaking into any important conversation, I could use a bit of help."

"I'm on my way down," the Pirate said. His voice echoed off the empty walls, the sound carrying through a series of tunnels and curves.

"Give me an end of your rope and I'll steady you as you descend," Pepe said to the Pirate.

"What do you need me to do?" Rita asked.

"Your job is to listen," the Pirate said to her. "We're not the only ones in these caves and tunnels. With any luck, there aren't more than a dozen others. But all will be looking for what we're looking for. Thanks to Pepe, we have a head start. But trust me, far behind us they're not."

"Nonna Maria should have made her way down to your boat by now," Rita said. "She told me she would wait for us there."

"That was my suggestion," Pepe the Painter said. "Otherwise, she would have been in here with us. And this foul air and slippery footing is no place for her. It was just a way to keep her involved and out of harm's way."

"She'll get to see all the boats on display and the outside of the castle on fire," the Pirate said, easing himself down the side of the cave. "She gets to enjoy the festival while we hunt for your grandfather's treasure."

The Pirate looked at the thick cord wrapped around Pepe the Painter's stomach. "I would feel much better if that rope were tied around a heavy boulder rather than your fat stomach," he said. "You sure you have enough strength in you to hold me?"

"If you go down, I'll be right behind you," Pepe said.

"In that case, I'll take my chances," the Pirate said. "Better to die with an old friend than to tumble down alone."

Pepe leaned against a cold wall and wrapped his hands around two breaks in the rock, the rope around his waist holding tight, swaying in the cave opening as the Pirate initiated his descent.

Within minutes, the Pirate was next to the Magician, watching as he swung a small pickax against a rock wall, a partial opening now exposed. "It never goes away, does it?" the Pirate asked him. "That feeling when you think you're close to what you're hoping to find."

"It's like your first kiss from the first girl to steal your heart," the Magician said. "It's the one memory that never fades."

"You think this is it?" the Pirate asked. "Paolino's hiding place?"

"It's someone's hiding place, that's for sure," the Magician said. "I've broken through enough of these to know that much. Now, whether it's gold or diamonds or just a small box filled with worthless coins, I can't tell you. But something's here. His map leads us right to this spot."

The Pirate looked at the piece of paper in the Magician's right hand. "I thought you gave Paolino's map to those pirates we ran into?" he said.

"I gave them *a* map," the Magician said. "I just didn't give them *the* map."

"We're also lucky Pepe found his sketches," the Pirate said. "I've heard about the House of Gold since I was old enough to swim the waters around these caves. I never thought I'd live to see it."

"That's one piece of a much larger puzzle, old friend," the Magician said, chipping away at the soft rock. "Even better than seeing it is putting our hands on what's buried inside the wet dirt. And this isn't the only soft ground down here. There are at least a dozen other places worth digging up."

"It's been more than a few years since we worked together," the Pirate said, smiling. "But I know that look in your eyes and the excitement in your voice. You have a plan, my friend. One that goes much deeper than looking for Paolino's hidden treasure."

The Magician stopped chipping away at the rock and turned to face the Pirate. "It's very simple, really," he said, lowering his voice to keep it from echoing through the cave opening. "Unless it's of great value, let the girl have whatever Paolino left behind. After all, it's her inheritance. We may be thieves. But we're not scoundrels."

"And then at some point, we come back down here and break through the other openings, and what we find we keep for ourselves," the Pirate said.

"Exactly," the Magician said. "We slice off a small portion for Pepe, since without his sketches it would have taken us months, if not years, to find the House of Gold."

"What about the others?" the Pirate asked. "I'm not as well known as you are. These days, I'm more a local curiosity than anything else, so no one will take much notice of what I do. But your reputation still causes certain hunters to raise an ear, especially if they hear you're back in the hunt."

"Word will get out," the Magician said. "There's no preventing that. Right now, as we're both down here, I would guess there are at least a dozen or so treasure hunters searching these caves, looking for whatever it is they think we're looking for. They've always been a step behind us, and they always will be. All except one."

The Pirate shook his head. "Not Emmitt Shaw," he said.

"He's the best one out there," the Magician said. "There's no other treasure hunter with his resources and skills. We'll need to come to an understanding with him if we decide to pursue this further."

"What kind of understanding?"

"He has resources that could be useful to us," the Magician said. "We'll offer him a percentage of whatever we manage to find. He does none of the work and pockets some of the profits.

Without any risk. That's something I think we can get him to sign off on."

"Where is he these days?" the Pirate asked. "You think with his money he wouldn't need to make a grab for any more than what he already has. Be happy living on his yacht on the Amalfi Coast or the French Riviera."

"He's here," the Magician said. "In Ischia. Probably in one of these caves, if I had to guess. Along with that woman he always works with. The one that always brought a smile to your face."

"Barbara Fay," the Pirate said.

"We'll work out the details in due time," the Magician said. "For now, let's keep looking for whatever Paolino thought was worth hiding inside this cave."

"Do you think he did?" the Pirate asked. "Hide anything worth hiding?"

The Magician turned and looked at the Pirate and nodded. "I wouldn't be down here if I didn't believe," he said. "And neither would you."

48.

LORETTA WALKED AT a brisk pace, turning the corner at Saint Peter's Church and down the incline that would eventually lead her to Nonna Maria's house. Her hands were bunched into tight fists and the lines along her forehead were deep and filled with concern. Her breath came out in a rush and her sleeveless blue dress was lined with sweat.

She made it down the incline and turned left, heading down the narrow walkway. Old stone houses lined one end, kitchen windows wide open, cooking smells filtering through the heavy, humid air. There was a low stone wall at the other end, a three-foot fence resting on unsteady thin poles running along the top, the thick, heavy growth of fig leaves blocking the view beyond.

Loretta wiped at her brow with her right arm, her thick strands of hair brushing against her eyes, her low-heeled shoes clicking and clacking along the cracked pavement. She stopped when she saw Il Presidente approaching her from the other end of the walkway.

"Is Nonna Maria home?" she shouted out to him. "Is she in her house?"

Il Presidente watched her for the briefest of moments, then

shook his head. "She told me she was going to the castle," he said, "to help some friends and then stay for the fireworks."

Loretta shook her head. "She's not there," she said. "I was supposed to meet her at the lower end, by the side of the small dock in Ischia Ponte."

"Why there?" Il Presidente asked.

"It's where the Pirate docked his boat for the night," Loretta said. "The boat was there, but she wasn't, and it's not like her to not be where she says she will be. Something's happened, Il Presidente. I'm certain of it. I think she's in trouble."

Il Presidente put his massive hands on Loretta's arms and stared into her eyes. "I'll go to the castle and look for her," he said. "Do you have your cell phone with you?"

Loretta nodded and reached into the pocket of her dress and took out an iPhone. "I would have called," she said, "but neither you nor Nonna Maria has a phone."

"Use your phone and get in touch with the captain," Il Presidente said. "Tell him what you told me and let him know I'm on my way down there."

"He might be in the area," Loretta said, "but none of his men are stationed there. I looked around for a carabiniere but there weren't any in front of the castle walkway or on the side streets of Ischia Ponte."

"Carabinieri aren't used for crowd control," Il Presidente said. "The municipal police handle that end, as you are aware. After you call the captain, text any friends you have who might be on duty. Ask them to keep an eye out for Nonna Maria."

"I was supposed to be working there tonight," she said. "But for the feast of Saint Anne, parking rules are ignored for the night, so I was given the night off."

"Tell the captain not to worry about Nonna Maria," Il Presidente said. "He has another matter he needs to focus on."

"I could come with you," Loretta said. "Help you find Nonna Maria. I can make the calls as we walk to the castle."

Il Presidente shook his head and turned and began a fast walk in the other direction. "I'll find her," he said. "Don't worry about that. I'll use the back roads to get to the castle. You go up Via Roma and make your way through the crowds. Meet up with me at the castle."

"How will you know where to look?" Loretta said, watching him make his way to Via Roma and the long walk to the castle. "She could be anywhere."

He stopped and looked back at Loretta. "It's what I do," he said.

Then Il Presidente turned and disappeared around a corner and into the thick crowd of tourists and locals.

49.

NICOLA SPAZZI RESTED his back against a stone wall in the shade of the pine garden near the entrance to the Bar Calise. He saw Captain Murino cross the busy four-way intersection, heading in his direction. The captain had a cell phone in his hand and his head down, gazing at the screen. The street in this area of the port was quiet, everyone either in Ischia Ponte or heading there to take in the fireworks display.

Spazzi waited as the captain walked past him, the gelateria to his left, the shuttered puppet theater to his right. He moved away from the wall and eased in several steps behind the captain. Spazzi was dressed in dark jeans, a black T-shirt, a thin leather jacket, and black boots. He had a gun nestled in the spine of his jeans and a serrated knife in a sheath resting against his right hip.

He approached the captain from behind, near the entrance to the remains of the old Jurassic Ischia, now a tree-shrouded runner's path. The captain was walking slowly and tapping a message on his cell phone.

Spazzi pulled the gun from his waistband, holding it low, and stepped closer to the captain, jamming the barrel into the center of his back. "Put the phone away and move toward the running path," Spazzi said to the captain. "We need to talk."

Captain Murino slid his cell phone into the front pocket of his uniform jacket and looked up at Spazzi. "I wondered about you from the day you first reported to headquarters," the captain said. "There was something off about you. But I must admit, you hid your true intentions. I never figured you for an assassin."

"I was trained well," Spazzi said. "And I devoted a great deal of time learning how not to give myself away. I've learned to adapt and wear many faces."

"And now, tonight, you show your real face," the captain said.

They were now walking along the running path, the thick line of trees offering them cover from any passersby in the street. "I had to learn how to be patient," Spazzi said. "To wait for the right time, the right place."

The captain stopped and glanced around at his surroundings and nodded. "It is an ideal spot," he said. "In the six years I've been here, this path has been used in the early morning by runners, myself among them. And by couples in love in the evening. And now, if what you intend to do to me happens, it will have its first murder."

"I would watch you on your morning runs," Spazzi said. "There was many a time I could have shot you, left you to bleed out, and been on my way."

"Why didn't you?"

"I wanted you to know who it was that was taking your life," Spazzi said. "I wanted you to see the smile on my face in the moments before you died."

"Joining the carabinieri, working with the department all this time, must have taken a great deal of planning," the captain said. "They do a deep dive into every candidate's background. Ostino must have shielded you all these years."

"We covered our tracks well," Spazzi said. "It took a long time, but looking at you now, I feel it was well worth the wait."

They were deep in the wooded area now, the dirt road lined with pine needles and cones. The only lights from the area were slivers of beams from the port and the Bar Calise in the distance. The captain waited until he heard the click of Spazzi's gun and then made his move. He dropped to one knee, turned, grabbed the hand holding the gun, and rammed it several times against the side of a tree. He shoved Spazzi's hand into the sharp edge of a broken branch, drawing blood and causing the gun to drop to the ground.

The captain rose to his feet, let go of Spazzi's hand, and landed two hard blows to the center of his chest. The punches caused Spazzi to gasp for air and bend at the waist. Spazzi reached for a handful of dirt and threw in in the captain's face, blinding him. He then jumped against the captain and the two fell to the ground, both tossing punches that landed on shoulders, faces, and back.

Spazzi rolled to his feet, reaching for the knife on his hip. He stopped when he heard footsteps and voices heading their way. In the distance, the night sky lit up with the start of the fireworks display.

The captain was on his feet, braced against the side of a tree, his uniform streaked with dust and dirt. "It looks as if you didn't plan everything as perfectly as you thought," the captain said. "You forgot about the carabinieri patrol. This is the time of night they check on the path. You should know that. You're the one who made the schedule."

Spazzi looked over his shoulder and spotted two shadows closing in. He looked at the captain and smiled. "The fun has just begun," he said.

He turned and ran off, heading toward the fireworks of Ischia Ponte and the feast of Saint Anne.

50.

THE MAGICIAN AND the Pirate walked slowly along the narrow ledge facing the open side of the cave, making their way down toward the entrance to the castle and the moored motorboat. Pepe the Painter and Rita were following close behind them. The Magician held a long dirt-stained sealed silver box under his right arm, gingerly feeling his way along the dark passageways.

"I have flashlights and flares in my backpack," Rita said, her voice echoing through the dark, empty space around them.

"I'm aware," the Magician said. "And we'll make use of them if needed. But I think it best we do not risk any unnecessary exposure to any other parties that may be in our vicinity."

"Especially now that we actually found something," the Pirate said.

"How do you know the box you found belonged to Paolino?" Pepe asked.

"I don't know it for a fact," the Magician said. "But the fact that we found it by following your sketches, which helped place us directly in the House of Gold, is one important clue."

"And the fact that it wasn't buried too far down in the

cave," the Pirate said. "Since I believe Paolino was on his own when he hid his box, he would try to stay as close to the upper edges as he could. Why risk dropping to his death if he could avoid it?"

"And there's no lock on the box," the Magician said. "That's one more important giveaway."

"What does that tell you?" Pepe the Painter asked.

"There are two kinds of ways to bury or hide treasure," the Pirate said. "One is, of course, by lock and key. And that was true, until the contraband years. We never locked whatever it was we kept hidden away. We sealed it."

"Why?" Rita asked.

"Well, for one thing, locks rust and, over time, break away on their own," the Magician said. "But even if that doesn't happen, it's never hard to crack open a lock."

"And combination locks are even worse, for my money," the Pirate said. "If someone knows enough to find a buried box, then that someone can figure a way to crack a combination."

"But if it's sealed, it's hard to open the box at the site," the Magician said. "It needs to be removed from where it was found. And there's plenty of risk to doing that."

"What kind of risk?" Rita asked.

"You can get caught before you have a chance to open it, for one," the Magician said. "And you can have it taken from you, either by the police or by a thief who might be tracking you and hanging back until you make a find."

The Magician rounded a tight corner and stopped; his eyes blinded by the harsh light from a high-beam flashlight aimed in his direction. "I prefer not to think of myself as a thief," the man holding the flashlight said.

He was hidden within the shadows of the cave, lines of smoke filtering down through the cracks from the castle fire around them. "Partner would be a much better description, and a more accurate one."

"Put down the light, Shaw," the Magician said. "It will attract attention we neither need nor want at this moment."

Shaw lowered the light and turned it off. He waited as the Magician and the others made their way to him, the sides of the cave growing wider the closer they got to the water's edge.

"I knew if anyone would discover anything other than old cartons of cigarettes and cases of stolen wine in these caves it would be you," Shaw said. "These others down here digging, and climbing, will be lucky if they can find their way out of the caves."

The Pirate moved in next to the Magician, keeping his eyes on Shaw. "Never thought I'd live to lay eyes on you again," he said.

Shaw nodded. "Never thought you'd live long enough," he said.

"Who is this man?" Pepe the Painter asked.

"I can answer that," Shaw said, taking several steps forward. "I'm the Magician's partner. And I suppose I'm yours as well. Which means half of what is in that silver box belongs to me."

The Pirate glared at the Magician. "So, it is true," he said. "You made a deal with him."

The Magician looked from Shaw to the Pirate. "I'm afraid I did," he said.

"And in our business, the deal we make is the deal we keep," Shaw said.

"That's true for the most part," the Magician said. "Unless a better deal is put on the table."

"And do you have a better deal?" Shaw asked.

"There's always a better deal," the Magician said.

51.

MARCO TOSSED AN empty water bottle into the thick foliage of the large garden and rubbed the back of his neck in frustration. "Nobody's coming for this old lady," he said to Carnale. "Nobody cares. She's a widow on an island filled with them."

"Did you hear that?" Carnale asked Nonna Maria. "You think that's true? That no one cares enough to come looking for you?"

Nonna Maria shrugged. "I'm sitting in the courtyard of what people tell me is a fancy and expensive restaurant," she said. "It's not the first place my friends would come looking."

"But you know your way around this castle," Carnale said. "Or so I've been led to believe."

"Anyone born on the island knows their way around the castle," Nonna Maria said.

"The stairwell is filled with smoke," Marco said. "Pretty soon we won't be able to see ten feet in front of us, and breathing is going to be a problem. We should leave the old woman and get out of here."

Nonna Maria looked down the length of the garden path and saw movement around the front gate. "The fireworks have started," she said. "And we can see it all from here. The smoke doesn't bother me. I'm used to it. My husband was a shepherd. He had fires going all the time on our property. It helped to keep the flock warm at night and safe from any animals looking to attack them."

Nonna Maria looked past Marco and Carnale at the looming presence of Il Presidente. He made no sound as he walked, the smoke filtering around his legs, his body shielded by shadows. He walked up the slight incline into the courtyard and waited as Marco and Carnale turned. He smiled when he saw the look in their eyes.

"How did you get in here?" Carnale managed to ask, when his initial shock wore off. "The front gate was locked. We had a key to get in. I don't think you did."

"You had a *stolen* key," Il President said. "I was given a key by a relative of the castle's owner."

"Who would that be?" Marco asked.

"He has my keys," Nonna Maria said. "Someone in my family owns the castle and was kind enough to give me a set of keys to the locked areas. That way, I could visit when the place isn't filled with tourists, as it is especially on a night like this one."

"Are you okay?" Il Presidente asked Nonna Maria, his eyes on Marco and Carnale. "Did they hurt you?"

"I wish they had hurt me," Nonna Maria said. "What they tried to do was even worse."

"What did they do?" Il Presidente asked.

"They wanted me to drink water," Nonna Maria said.

She stood up from the chair and walked over toward Il Presidente, the large black tote bag in her right hand. Marco pulled a knife from under his shirt pocket and reached out his free hand, looking to grab Nonna Maria.

Il Presidente blocked his path and held the hand holding the knife. With one smooth, fast move, he snapped Marco's hand back, hard enough to snap bone. Marco slid to his knees, and two swift blows from Il Presidente's closed fist sent him flat on his face.

Nonna Maria watched Carnale circle behind Il Presidente. She grabbed the large bottle of water resting on top of the table, eased in behind Carnale, and swung the bottle against the side of his face, watching as he tumbled to the ground. The bottle fell from her hand and shattered on the hard stones of the garden path.

Il Presidente turned to Nonna Maria and smiled. "I'm glad you found some use for the water."

Nonna Maria nodded. "It's good for cooking pasta and soups," she said. "And for helping plants grow. And now for knocking criminals off their feet."

Carnale stood up on shaky legs, blood running down the side of his face, and moved toward Il Presidente, both hands balled into fists. "Don't try me," Il Presidente said to him. "If Nonna Maria knocked you off your feet, take a minute and think what I'll do to you."

"I just want to get off this island," Carnale said.

Il Presidente moved toward Carnale. "We can help you and your partner on the ground," he said. "But before we do, I want to know why the man sent here to kill the captain has waited this long to make his move."

"I only know what I was told," Carnale said.

"Then tell us that," Il Presidente said.

"Ostino was sentenced to life in prison eight years ago," Carnale said. "And the assassin marked the day he was sent away as the day he would take the captain's life."

Nonna Maria walked over to Carnale, took a folded handkerchief from the front pocket of her black blouse, and gently wiped the blood flowing down the side of his face. "What day was it?" she said in a soft voice. "Please."

Carnale looked at Nonna Maria. "Today," he said. "July twenty-sixth."

52.

NICOLA SPAZZI MOVED through the dense crowd of tourists and locals cramming the streets of Ischia Ponte. Captain Murino was a dozen feet behind him in hot pursuit. Overhead, the fireworks display continued to light up the sparkling star-filled sky.

Spazzi scooted past the bookstore, moving to his left, the castle looming in the near distance. The captain couldn't risk an altercation with Spazzi on the crowded streets. He couldn't be certain Spazzi didn't have another weapon in his possession and was not eager to get in a firefight surrounded by so many innocent civilians. He would also figure that Spazzi would want to take him on one on one, and the best place for that would be the empty castle, now less than half a mile away.

Spazzi turned and caught Murino's eye and smiled. He felt certain he once again had the carabiniere at a disadvantage, looking to bring him to higher ground, trusting his judgment that when it came to a fight to the death, he was by far the better of the two. He had devoted the bulk of his life to such confrontations. Plus, he had a fueling motive the captain lacked. Revenge.

Both Spazzi and the captain ran past teenagers and children sitting on the thick black rocks bordering both sides of the walkway, some with their feet dangling in the water, others swaying to songs sung by an assortment of local talent, led by Aldo Poli, Ischia's favorite singer.

Captain Murino's phone vibrated, and he took it out of a side pocket of his pants and glanced down at the text. It was a second one from Loretta. She was nearing the castle entrance and there was still no sign of Nonna Maria. The captain texted a reply, alerting her that Spazzi was in the vicinity. He also wrote that if anyone could find Nonna Maria and keep her from harm, it would be Il Presidente.

The captain returned the cell phone to his pocket, looked through the crowd, and spotted Spazzi running up the first flight of castle steps. The assassin was looking for the perfect place to have their final confrontation. And Captain Murino could think of no better place than the medieval torture museum, on the third tier of the castle.

The captain slowed his walk as he neared the castle steps. He glanced out at the bay, still crowded with boats decked out in a variety of colors. The fireworks above were edging toward their grand finale, and the smoke from the burning wood placed around the castle gave the imposing structure an ominous appearance. It was, in so many ways, the perfect setting for the final battle in a war the captain had started eight years ago.

53.

IL PRESIDENTE LED Marco and Carnale out the front gate of the
Monastery. Nonna Maria waited until they came out, then took
the key from Il Presidente and locked the gate. She put the keys
in the pocket of her blouse, reached for her black tote bag, and
turned toward Il Presidente. "You told them where to meet us?"
she asked him.

Il Presidente nodded. "They should be around the next
bend," he said. "Their boat is moored at the small dock near
the castle."

"Where do you plan to take us?" Carnale asked.

"It's time for you both to leave Ischia," Nonna Maria said.
"Since the commercial boats have shut down for the night, two
friends of ours have agreed to take you to Naples."

"We can wait until morning," Carnale said.

"We won't be of any help to you if you wait till the sun rises,"
Il Presidente said. "You won't be allowed off the island. Instead,
the two of you will be arrested by the carabinieri and charged
with kidnapping and held in the local jail."

"It will be better if you go with my friends to Naples," Nonna
Maria said. "The boat they have is not big, but they will give
you food and wine and make you comfortable."

"The prison boat is not a boat you want to be on," Il Presidente said. "I speak from experience."

"What happens once we're in Naples?" Marco managed to ask, speaking through gritted teeth, his wrist swollen and painful.

"That part is out of our hands," Il Presidente said. "If you're lucky, you'll make your way back to where you came from. And that will be the end of your adventure. But word in our world travels without sound. You took a job and came here without permission from the man you should have asked. Whether you were decoys in the plan won't matter to him. It's about respect, and you didn't show him any. And for that there is always a price."

Il Presidente led them down the steps and around a sharp bend, down to the dock near the local beach in Ischia Ponte. They stopped in front of a small motorboat. Two women, Claudia and Annarella, dressed in black, were sitting in either end. The engine was running, and both nodded at Nonna Maria and Il Presidente.

"You'll be safe with them," Nonna Maria said to Carnale and Marco. "They will cause you no harm."

One of the Mourners stepped out of the boat and helped the injured Marco step on, the waves rocking the craft back and forth. Then she turned and waited for Carnale to get on board. He turned and looked at Nonna Maria.

"I suppose I owe you an apology, old woman," he said.

Nonna Maria shook her head. "You don't owe me anything," she said.

She stepped back and watched as Il Presidente tossed the thick rope from the mooring onto the stern of the motorboat.

They stood at the dock and waited as the motorboat, slowly and skillfully, navigated around the bay crowded with boats big and small, and made its way to open sea.

"Think they'll make it out of Naples?" Nonna Maria asked. "Back to their home city?"

Il Presidente shrugged. "Maybe," he said. "They might not be a big enough target for Monte. They just took orders. He might want to wait and strike at the one who gave that order. Why go after small fish when the big fish still waits to be caught?"

"Leave the rabbits and wait for the fox," Nonna Maria said.

"Something like that," Il Presidente said, smiling.

"I don't think I could have survived in that world," Nonna Maria said. "Life and death are decided in the same way I decide what to prepare for a meal. Your best friend today is your enemy tomorrow. It's not the way a life should be lived."

"Probably not," Il Presidente said. "But sometimes it is the only choice a man is given."

Nonna Maria looked at Il Presidente and nodded. "I know," she said.

"You want to go and sit by Coco's and watch the end of the fireworks?" Il Presidente asked.

"Our night's not over yet," she said. "We must find the captain."

"Loretta went looking for him," Il Presidente said. "They can't be far."

"Where would you lead the captain?" Nonna Maria asked. "If you had been the one chosen to end his life?"

"Here," he said. "Into the castle. In the medieval museum, or down in the Cemetery of Dead Nuns."

"Then that's where we go," Nonna Maria said. She turned and started back up the steps toward the middle tier of the castle.

"This is one thing I never thought I would do," Il Presidente said, following close behind.

"Take me to the feast?" Nonna Maria said.

"Not that," Il Presidente said.

"Then what?"

"Rush to the aid of a carabinieri captain," Il Presidente said. "Given the life I've led."

"Don't think of it as helping a carabinieri captain," Nonna Maria said.

"How should I think of it?"

"Saving the life of a friend," Nonna Maria said.

54.

THE MAGICIAN SAT across from Shaw and Barbara Fay. The Pirate sat next to him, Rita by his side. Pepe the Painter leaned his back against an iron railing, his arms folded across his chest. They were at a corner table in Da Salvatore's restaurant, bottles of mineral water and red and white wine and glasses crowding the small table. Three lit candles rested alongside the wine and water bottles. The waves from the nearby beach splattered against the sides of the thick rocks lining both sides of the restaurant. The shadow of the castle, the fires outside still aflame, hovered over them.

"Is this your place?" Shaw asked the Magician.

The Magician shook his head. "Belongs to an old friend," he said. "But he and his son let us use it if we need a quiet place."

"They only open for lunch," the Pirate said. "So sometimes I dock my motorboat out there and sit at one of these tables. If they know I'm coming, they always leave a meal for me to enjoy in the kitchen."

"You have a key, then?" Shaw said.

"No," the Pirate said. "This place has been here for more decades than I can remember, and that glass door is never locked."

"I get it," Barbara said. "It's a safe place for us to talk. So, then, let's talk."

The Pirate took a long drink of white wine and smiled at Barbara. "I could get to like you," he said.

"Save yourself time," Barbara said. "I make it a rule never to go out with a man who doesn't wear pants or a shirt. I know I'm picky, but there it is."

"Back in the caves, you mentioned a better deal," Shaw said to the Magician. "Now would be a good time to hear it."

"It's simple enough," the Magician said. "Pepe has made sketches of the inside of the caves and tunnels and, along with me, knows its history as well as anyone you'll find on the island or in any university in Europe. He studied it for decades and paints it every day and night."

Shaw looked up at Pepe the Painter. "And what have you learned in all those years, other than what colors to paint the castle?"

Pepe took a deep breath and looked at Shaw and Fay for a few moments. "There's quite a bit hidden inside those caves," he said. "Most of it worth nothing or very little. Some of it worth a fortune."

"You've known this for a long time, yet not done anything about it," Fay said. "Why is that?"

"It's not what I'm interested in," Pepe the Painter said. "I'm not a treasure hunter like the rest of you. That castle to me is an old and trusted friend. I am happiest when I'm in there or when I'm painting its walls and towers."

"Go on," Shaw said to the Magician.

"You and Barbara go back on your boat, travel to some of the islands, enjoy some leisure time," the Magician said. "Once they see you leave, these other treasure hunters will figure you either found what you were looking for or gave up the search. Either way, they'll go looking somewhere else for their treasure."

"We can spread rumors there's something to be found along the Amalfi Coast," the Pirate said. "Something like that might get them moving a lot faster."

"And what happens when we come back from our little vacation?" Barbara asked.

"We sit down, we study Pepe's sketches and his books and get to know the ins and outs of that castle almost as well as he does," the Magician said. "And then we go in and start hunting treasure. On our own, with no one else in the mix."

"And we split whatever we find how?" Shaw asked.

"Even cuts between me, you, Barbara, and the Pirate," the Magician said. "Pepe gets a finder's fee for any discovery. And Rita here leaves with the box we found. The one we believe belonged to her grandfather."

"Before we agree, how about we open the box and see what he left her?" Shaw asked.

The Magician shook his head. "That doesn't get opened here," he said.

"And why is that?" Barbara asked.

"You know the rules, Barbara, better than I do," the Magician said. "It needs to be opened in the presence of the person who hired me to help find it. And that's not you or Shaw."

"You think we'll find any treasure inside those caves?" Shaw asked.

"Maybe," the Magician said. "Maybe not. But it would be fun to try, and it would be truly amazing if we did."

"It will be our last big hunt," the Pirate said. "At least it will be mine. And I can't think of doing it with better company."

"And since none of us trust one another," the Magician said, "I can't think of a more perfect partnership."

Shaw shook his head and laughed. "Neither can I," he said. "We have a deal."

The Pirate left the table, went through the open glass door of the restaurant, and came out with three open bottles of white wine. He sat back down, rested two of the bottles on the table, and poured wine into five glasses from the third. "Let's seal it with a toast," he said, raising his glass.

"To lost treasures and untrustworthy friends," the Magician said, his glass filled with mineral water.

They clinked glasses and drank.

The Pirate looked at Barbara and smiled. She looked back at him and waved him away. "You can dream, Pirate," she said, not bothering to hide her smile. "But that's all it would be. A dream."

"A dream, a boat, and a bottle of cold wine is all I want or need," the Pirate said.

"And a few trunks filled with lost treasure to load into that boat," the Magician said.

"That's a picture I would love to paint," Pepe the Painter said.

55.

CAPTAIN MURINO AND Nicola Spazzi stood facing each other in the center of the medieval torture museum. "I figured this would be where I would find you," the captain said. "A few of the men mentioned how often you come up here, usually on your lunch break."

Spazzi nodded and gazed around the room. "I'm fascinated with the methods people long ago used to exact their revenge against an opponent," he said. "And I always felt this would be the perfect place for me to finally take you down after all these years."

"I took Ostino down more than eight years ago," the captain said. "It must have eaten at you to have to wait all this time to come after me."

Spazzi shook his head. "On the contrary," he said. "It needed to be planned out and executed to perfection. And that required a great deal of time. I needed to learn my trade, go up against lesser men, and then work it so I could get close to you. It does require a great deal of patience, but in the end, standing here now, facing you, I realize it was well worth it."

"I have to admit, becoming a member of the carabinieri had a touch of brilliance to it," the captain said. "That's why it took me so long to piece it together. And even then I had my doubts."

"If you must know the truth, it sickened me to wear that uniform all these years," Spazzi said. "To be a member of a group I learned long ago to despise."

Behind them, on the streets below, the throngs of people were still in full celebration, while above them the night sky sparkled under a large blanket of stars.

"I can't wait to be rid of that uniform," Spazzi said. "I'll burn it the first chance I get."

"So, despite the disgust you felt, you pretended to be my friend," Captain Murino said. "But you overplayed your hand a bit. I never put much faith in your carefully chosen words. The flattery, the false admiration, the reasons behind wanting to come to Ischia, just to work by my side, to learn from me. That I found hard to believe."

"Yet you did nothing about it?" Spazzi said.

"That's not quite true," the captain said. "I got in touch with some friends in Florence and they dug into your background. It took them a while, since you were clever enough not to leave much of a paper trail. But they managed to put together some of the pieces."

"Which explains why you never seemed concerned about the men I wanted you to think were on the island to do you harm," Spazzi said.

"There are still some holes in your story to fill," the captain said.

"I can help with that," Spazzi said. "I am a real carabiniere, trained and schooled as you were. But unlike you, I never planned to make a career of it."

"And was I always your sole target?" the captain asked.

"Don't flatter yourself, Captain," Spazzi said. "There were a few members of your team that were targeted early. Three of them, in fact. I used them for practice, to make sure my ruse would not be discovered. But you were the one I most wanted."

"You're a damaged man, Spazzi," Captain Murino said. "It is easy for me to see why Ostino chose you for this mission. You dedicated years of your life to reach this moment. All on the word of a man who would not care one bit whether you lived or died."

Spazzi laughed, the sound echoing off the thick stone walls. "Is that what you think?" he asked. "That I was chosen by Ostino to join the carabinieri and somehow, some way, find my way to you? Truth is, Ostino was against my plan and asked me several times, in person and through intermediaries, to not go through with it."

"So why did you, then?"

"I love the man," Spazzi said. "My mother was one of his many lovers, but the one he cared about the most. When she died at a young age, he could have turned his back on me. Instead, he took me in, raised me as his own. He thinks of me as a son. And he's the only father I've ever known."

"A father who teaches the young man he claims to love how to kill," the captain said. "How to ruin lives. How to get his revenge. Tell me, Spazzi, what kind of father is that?"

"He's an enemy only to you," Spazzi said. "Not to me."

Captain Murino nodded and glanced around at the various weapons encased behind glass. "In that case, there's only one thing left for us to do."

Spazzi smiled. "Finally, we are in agreement," he said.

56.

IL PRESIDENTE AND Nonna Maria had their backs against a stone wall, just around the bend from the entrance to the torture museum. "They just went in," he said in a near whisper. "I don't suppose I can persuade you to wait here or, even better, wait for me on the walkway? It will make what I may need to do much easier."

"I can't leave you now," Nonna Maria said. "There's going to be trouble in that museum, and you might need my help."

"The captain will need to keep his focus on Spazzi," Il Presidente said.

"We need to keep an eye out for Loretta," Nonna Maria said. "She'll find her way to us somehow. She won't be content to wait down by the entrance."

"You go in first," Il Presidente said. "Spazzi must have heard by now that his two decoys took you hostage, but he might be very surprised to see you still at the castle."

"He will see me as one more problem for the captain," Nonna Maria said.

"That's right," Il Presidente said. "But he won't be expecting me to be there. I'll come in after you. If it goes our way,

Spazzi will want to go to the second floor. That's where the lethal weapons are kept."

"And that's where you will help the captain fight Spazzi?" Nonna Maria asked.

"No," Il Presidente said. "That's where I get you out of Spazzi's reach. It is up to the captain to take on Spazzi. It's the way he would want it and it's the way it should be. I'm not part of their history."

"Spazzi is here to kill the captain," Nonna Maria said. "He doesn't just want to beat him in a fight. I can't let that happen."

Il President stayed silent for a moment, then looked at Nonna Maria and nodded. "If it gets that far, I'll bring a stop to it. But I must be honest, if I do, it will be a first for me."

"You've broken up fights before," Nonna Maria said. "I've seen you do it a few times myself."

"But I have never stepped in between two carabinieri," Il Presidente said. "It goes against the code I used to live by."

Nonna Maria smiled. "You're living under a different code now," she said.

57.

THE TORTURE MUSEUM had been in the castle for five hundred years. There were weapons displays spread across two floors and a brief history of the uses of each written on placards beneath each one. Many of the weapons were given colorful names—from the Head Crusher to Eye Spoons—and there was even a functioning guillotine along with a variety of instruments designed to maim and dismember an enemy. The displays were kept locked behind glass panels. The halls were narrow, and one of the stairwells led down to the Cemetery of Dead Nuns.

Captain Murino stood with his back against a display case filled with knives of various shapes and sizes. He looked across the room at Spazzi and saw him direct his attention to an open door to his left. Spazzi smiled when he saw Loretta standing there. He reached out a hand and dragged Loretta toward him, wrapping an arm around her waist and holding her tight against him.

"Now it looks as if we have ourselves a party," he said to the captain.

"Let her go," Murino said to him. "You won't get satisfaction taking your revenge on Loretta. It's me you should be fighting, me you need to finish. I'm your only path to vengeance."

"Maybe," Spazzi said. "But if I harm your Loretta, I leave behind a ruined man."

"A ruined man who will not stop until he kills you," the captain said. "I'm the one you want and the one you need to take down."

"And while we're doing battle, what do you propose I do with Loretta?" Spazzi asked.

"I'll take care of her," Nonna Maria said from the stairwell behind Spazzi.

Spazzi swung Loretta around until they were both facing Nonna Maria. "You are always where you shouldn't be, old woman," he said to her.

"My family owns this castle," Nonna Maria said. "I can come and go as I please."

Captain Murino looked to his left, Spazzi now with his back to him, and spotted Il Presidente stepping into the room, coming in through another stairwell. He nodded at the captain and then in one swift motion grabbed Spazzi by the neck of his uniform collar and yanked him backward. The move caught Spazzi off guard and was enough to free his hold on Loretta.

Spazzi turned and reached for a wooden mallet resting against a corner wall. He swung it at Il Presidente, the blow glancing off his shoulder and sending him tumbling backward. Spazzi raised the mallet, but before he could land another blow against Il Presidente he was knocked off balance by a punch to his back from Captain Murino, hard enough to send Spazzi to his knees and force him to drop the weapon.

"Get Loretta and Nonna Maria out of here," the captain said to Il Presidente. "This is between me and Spazzi."

Il Presidente regained his footing and turned to Loretta and

Nonna Maria. "Go," he said to them. "Both of you. We'll meet by the entrance to the castle."

"What about the captain?" Loretta asked.

Il Presidente glanced at Spazzi and the captain, circling each other, eyes focused, hands balled into fists. "He has business he needs to take care of," he said. "He'll come down when he's finished."

Spazzi glared at both Murino and Il Presidente. "The two of you against me," he said. "That was the plan all along. You knew you weren't good enough to take me on by yourself."

"This is between us, Spazzi," the captain said.

Il Presidente nodded at the captain and stared at Spazzi. "It's a shame, you know," Spazzi said to him. "You and I have much in common. We should be fighting on the same side."

"We have nothing in common," Il Presidente said as he walked out of the room. "And we were never on the same side."

58.

NONNA MARIA AND Loretta walked out of the museum and stood against the stone wall next to the entrance.

"Are you hurt?" Nonna Maria asked.

Loretta shook her head. "Just a bit bruised from his hold on me," she said. "But I am terrified for Paolo."

"Captain Murino and Spazzi need to bring it to an end," Nonna Maria said. "But he won't be alone."

"But Il Presidente told us to go down to the castle entrance," Loretta said, "and he'd meet us there."

"That wasn't meant for our ears," Nonna Maria said. "That was so Spazzi would think he and the captain were the only ones left in the castle."

"So where will he be going?" Loretta asked.

"One floor below," Nonna Maria said. "To the Cemetery of Dead Nuns. That's where Il Presidente will be waiting."

"Why there?"

"The museum steps lead to it," Nonna Maria said.

"I'm afraid for him, Nonna Maria," Loretta said. "Spazzi is out for blood. And Paolo has been in Ischia for so long, I worry he has lost that instinct, that edge that made him what he was during his years in Florence."

"The captain has not shown that side in Ischia because he hasn't had to," Nonna Maria said. "But that part of him never goes away. It didn't for Il Presidente after those many years living as he did. And it hasn't left the captain. It's a part of who he is and who he will always be. And it's a part of the man you love."

"I hope that's true, Nonna Maria," Loretta said.

Nonna Maria nodded. "I hope so too," she said.

59.

"I HAVE HUNGERED for this moment for a long time," Spazzi said to the captain.

"Then don't waste it," the captain said.

They stood facing each other in the center of the room, surrounded by lethal medieval weapons, their hands at their sides, their bodies tense. Spazzi made the first move. He rushed the captain, catching him at chest level and shoving him against a glass panel. The panel shook but didn't break.

Captain Murino raised his right knee and landed a hard blow to Spazzi's stomach. Murino then tossed Spazzi to the ground, the back of his head bouncing off stone.

Spazzi slid his right hand down to his belt, reaching for his revolver. Murino stepped forward and slammed his foot down on Spazzi's hand, then leaned over and pulled the weapon free and tossed it into a corner of the room. Murino rested his shoulders against a pane of glass and allowed himself a moment to catch his breath. Spazzi got to his knees. He reached out a hand and braced it against the side of a wall and managed to get back on his feet, standing on shaky legs.

Spazzi mustered all the strength he had and charged Murino, catching him off guard and slamming his head against a glass pane, shattering it into shards. He ripped a broken piece of glass from the panel, cutting the palm of his hand as he did. He swung it at Murino and caught the captain above the right shoulder, shredding his uniform jacket and cutting through skin.

Spazzi dropped the shard of glass and swung two hard punches at the captain, the first catching him on the side of the face, the second hitting nothing but air. The blow sent the captain tumbling backward, knocking over a wooden stand. As Spazzi came in closer, Murino wrapped his arms around him and swung him to the ground. They both fell against the stone pavement, Murino landing face-first, Spazzi on his back.

Spazzi rose and headed for the stairwell, making his way to the Cemetery of Dead Nuns. Murino got to his feet, arm numb, face throbbing, and chased after Spazzi.

As Murino reached the bottom of the stairs, he saw Spazzi standing between two stone chairs, the final resting places of nuns who had died centuries earlier.

Spazzi smiled when he saw the captain. "I'll leave you as they were left, sitting up and bleeding out," Spazzi said.

"I much prefer their company to yours," Captain Murino said.

Spazzi began to circle the captain. Murino swung first and landed a right against Spazzi's rib cage. Spazzi countered with three hooks to Murino's wounded shoulder, his arm dangling against his waist.

A Spazzi left grazed Murino's face. Murino ducked under another wild swing, rammed his head against Spazzi's chest, and followed that with several blows to his stomach. Spazzi fell to his knees, unable to catch his breath. Murino shoved Spazzi against a corner of one of the stone chairs.

Murino grabbed Spazzi's head and rested it in the center of a stone chair. The captain dropped to his knees, straddling Spazzi's chest. He lifted the assassin's head, ready to slam it against the stone chair.

"Don't," Nonna Maria said. She stepped out of the shadows and stood facing the captain. "You don't want to kill him."

Captain Murino looked up at Nonna Maria, his eyes still gleaming with a fighter's anger, his body tense and coiled, his wounds oozing blood. "He would have left me here to die," he said to her, not seeming a bit surprised to see her down in the cemetery.

"That's the kind of man Spazzi is," Nonna Maria said. "If you kill him, you will be the same kind of man. And I don't think that's who you are."

Captain Murino stared at Nonna Maria for several moments and then released his grip on Spazzi's head. "And what kind of man is that, Nonna Maria?" he asked.

"A better man," Nonna Maria said.

Captain Murino looked down at the dazed and bleeding Spazzi. "You won't die tonight, Spazzi," the captain said. "Not here. Not on this island. You will be sent to where you belong. Behind the bars of a prison cell. And for the rest of your days, you'll see as much sunlight as the poor nuns buried here."

Murino got to his feet and tried to lift Spazzi. His wounded right arm wasn't strong enough to lift him and he leaned against a stone wall for support. Il Presidente came out from the shadows. He reached down and lifted Spazzi to his feet. Captain Murino looked at him and smiled. "Would you like to cuff him for me?" he asked.

Il Presidente returned the smile. "This is a night of firsts for me," he said. "Maybe just this one time. I wouldn't want word to get around I'm working with the carabinieri."

"It's our secret," Captain Murino said, handing Il Presidente a set of handcuffs.

Il Presidente swung Spazzi around and slammed the cuffs tight around his wrists. "I'll drag him down to the castle entrance," he said. "We'll wait for you there."

Nonna Maria rested a hand on Captain Murino's good arm. "I'll go with him," she said. "I won't be much help getting you out of here. I have a bad hip and a heavy tote bag."

Captain Murino reached down and kissed Nonna Maria on her cheek. "Don't worry about me, I'll be fine," he said.

"I know," Nonna Maria said. "Loretta is here to make sure of that."

Captain Murino turned and saw Loretta, tears in her eyes and a smile on her face.

"What are you doing in here?" he asked.

"What we were all doing, Captain," Nonna Maria said. "She was here helping a friend. In her case, a friend she loves and plans to marry."

60.

NONNA MARIA SAT across from Rita, the long silver box resting on the table between them. The Magician and the Pirate sat at the head of the table, their chairs braced against each other. Pepe the Painter stood with his back against the wall leading to the kitchen.

Rita stared down at the silver box. "I knew it was my grandfather's the second I saw it," she said.

"The drawing of the snake head on top of the box," the Pirate said. "Paolino had a fondness for snakes. From the time he was a boy. Not sure where that came from. There are hardly any snakes on the island."

"If you're ready," Nonna Maria said to Rita, "the Magician brought some tools to help open the box."

Rita turned to the Magician and nodded. The Magician pushed his seat back, leaned over, and eased the silver box closer to him. He reached down and picked up a coil of leather and unfurled it. He looked down at the array of instruments lined up in the leather pouch and picked up a small hammer and a flat blade with a wooden handle. He jammed the blade under one side of the silver box and gently tapped it with the hammer. After several blows, the lid began to loosen. He pulled the blade out, turned the box around, and repeated the actions on the other side. He then put down the blade and hammer and slid the silver box toward Rita.

"It is ready to be opened," he said.

Rita gently eased the top off the silver box and rested it on the table. Then they looked inside and remained silent for several moments that felt like the passing of a day.

Inside were a drawing of a beautiful woman, her head covered by a long blue veil; three pieces of jewelry; a chiseled crucifix; and three folded pieces of parchment.

"The drawing is of Vittoria Colonna, the Marchese di Pescara," Pepe the Painter said. "She was a poet who lived here in Ischia for many years. In the castle. The main street of Ischia Porto is named for her."

"She was a widow and a patron of Michelangelo," the Pirate said. "It was said he was in love with her; not sure if that's just legend. But he did come here and built a house directly across from the castle. He would gaze across the bay and look at her through the windows."

"Do you know where the jewels and the crucifix are from?" Rita asked.

"The three pieces each have a history. They were given to Vittoria Colonna as a wedding gift from her husband," the Magician said. "They had been given to him by his mother."

"So, she lived with her husband in the castle?" Rita asked.

"Sadly, no," Pepe the Painter said. "He died young, in battle, somewhere in Spain. She remained a widow the rest of her days."

"That first piece, the small diamond cross on a gold chain, is a sign of his love for her," the Magician said. "The second piece, the ruby, diamond, and emerald set in gold, means she will always have his heart. And that final piece is the mystery piece many have been seeking for decades. It's called a Desciogch, and it is worth a great deal of money."

"Why that one?" Rita asked.

"For the simple reason that there aren't many of them in the world," the Magician said. "And over time, a mystery has grown around such a piece. What does it mean, where is it from, who made it?"

"And the crucifix?" Rita whispered.

"That is the greatest gift of all," the Pirate said. "It was made by Michelangelo and given to Vittoria Colonna as a gift to show his appreciation for her many years of patronage."

Rita unfolded one of the pieces of parchment, looked at it for a moment, then read it aloud. "It's in my grandfather's hand," she said. "It's a copy of a note Vittoria Colonna wrote to Michelangelo after he sent her the crucifix. She wrote, 'When I saw it, it so surpassed my expectations in every way, I could not possibly have wished for more.'"

"Paolino loved you very much," Nonna Maria said. "And the gifts he left you mean more than diamonds and rubies and a crucifix made by Michelangelo's own hands. Like Vittoria Colonna's husband, Paolino left you his heart, his soul, and the possessions that meant so much to him. What he most loved and cherished, he left to the one he most loved and cherished."

Rita wiped tears from her eyes and looked at the four faces around her. "I know he did," she said. "And I would never have found any of them without your help. I don't know how to thank you."

"Secure them in a safe place," Pepe the Painter said. "Unless you plan to sell them."

"The Michelangelo and the Desciogch are probably worth the most," the Pirate said. "But the others have great value as well."

"I will never sell them," Rita said. "They will always stay with me. It's what he would have wanted. And even more, it's what I want."

"If you need a secure place to store them, we can help you," Pepe the Painter said.

"I know exactly where I want them kept," Rita said.

"Where?" the Magician asked.

"In Vittoria Colonna's home," Rita said. "The castle. These gifts are hers as much as they are mine. The jewels she was given by her husband and the crucifixion done by Michelangelo. They belong to both of us. Can you find a place inside the castle where they will be safe and where I can go see them whenever I want?"

The three men exchanged a quick glance and a smile. "We'll find a place," the Magician said. "We'll do it together, and we'll make it easy for you to access but at the same time keep them out of public view."

"Anywhere but in one of those caves," Nonna Maria said. "My days inside those caves are behind me."

"Are you certain, Nonna Maria?" the Pirate asked. "There's a lot more treasure to be found inside those caves."

"You already have a partner," Nonna Maria said. "You don't need another."

"How do you know that?" the Magician asked. "About our partner?"

"Shaw has been coming to Ischia for many summers," Nonna Maria said. "And he's always been fascinated with what might be hidden inside those caves. He just needed the right people to help him search for it. And now, with the three of you, he finally has what he needs. You'll get more help from him than you ever would from me."

"You know, it's not only lost treasure that might be hidden in those caves," the Pirate said. "There might also be hundreds of cases of wine hidden there. From the contraband years. The best wines, kept cool all these years inside those caves."

Nonna Maria poured herself a fresh cup of coffee and smiled. "Now," she said, "that's my idea of a lost treasure."

61.

NONNA MARIA STARED out her kitchen window at the big tables spread out in her courtyard, plates, silverware, glasses, carafes filled with chilled wine, and sweaty bottles of mineral water dotting each table. The oven and grills downstairs were being manned by Giovanni the taxi driver and Il Presidente, who were in charge of making a variety of pizzas, breads, lemon chicken, and fish marinated in herbs, lemon, and olive oil.

Nonna oversaw the rest. Her kitchen overflowed with enormous platters of eggplant parmigiana, veal cutlet and arugula in a lemon and oil dressing, stuffed peppers, marinated artichokes, sauteed escarole stuffed with pine nuts, capers, and anchovies, roasted chickens stuffed with hot cherry peppers and olives, string beans dressed in olive oil, garlic, and red wine vinegar, sauteed cabbage, roasted zucchini dressed in herbs and vinegar, and a large tomato and red onion salad with cucumbers and goat cheese. The desserts would arrive later in the day, delivered fresh from Minicucci's bakery.

Several of her grandchildren and great-grandchildren were helping to set out the chairs and arrange the seating. Nonna Maria turned away from the window and smiled when she saw Loretta standing at the kitchen entrance. "I can't thank you enough for doing this," Loretta said. "Paolo and I did have an engagement party, but nothing like this feast you have prepared."

"It's as much for me as it is for you," Nonna Maria said. "I miss cooking big meals. My Gabriel loved having our friends and family here, eating, drinking, laughing, and singing. All the people we loved and cared about in one place. It was the life we had built surrounding us."

Loretta stepped closer to Nonna Maria and embraced her and held her for several moments. When she released her, there were tears in both their eyes. "I feel the same as you do, little one," Nonna Maria said. "We don't always need words to tell someone what they mean to us."

"I hear voices coming down the courtyard," Loretta said, wiping away her tears.

"And if I know my friends and family as well as I think I do, those are hungry mouths that will need to be fed," Nonna Maria said. "It's a special day for two very special people."

"Do you need help with anything?" Loretta asked, looking around the crowded kitchen.

"There's very little for me to do," Nonna Maria said. "The stove does the hard work. And the children come up and take down the dishes. You go and enjoy the party. I'll be there as soon as the coffee is ready."

They all came to celebrate. All Nonna's adult children, teasing and laughing and at ease in one another's company. And as many of her friends as she could cram into the courtyard and the two floors of her home. Pepe the Painter; her nephew, Agostino, the doctor; Captain Murino, his fiancée, Loretta, by his side; Gennaro, Loretta's father, and Andrea, her mother; Rita; the

Magician; the Pirate; two of the Mourners, Claudia and Annarella; Antonio and Branka from the Excelsior. Even Shaw and Barbara Fay were there to celebrate.

Nonna Maria was sitting at her dining room table, a cup of espresso by her right elbow, looking up at the framed photo of her husband, Gabriel. She sipped the coffee and smiled.

Captain Murino walked into the room and sat across from her. He reached for her hand. "Thank you," he said. "Not just for this day, but for every day that you've been my friend. I've had many partners in my years as a carabiniere, especially in my time in the North. But I've never had a better one than you. And I know I'll never have a better friend."

"You're wrong, Captain," Nonna Maria said. "Loretta will be the best friend you will ever have. She loves you as I loved my Gabriel, and there isn't much more we can ask than that."

Il Presidente walked into the room, carrying a large box of pastries. "The kid from the bakery just delivered these," he said. "I'll put them in the kitchen." He rested a hand on Nonna Maria's shoulder as he walked past. She grabbed his hand and held it. Captain Murino looked at Il Presidente. "I appreciate all the help you gave me these past few days," he said. "I'm not sure I would have made it without you."

Il Presidente looked at the captain for a moment and then at Nonna Maria. "I didn't help you because you were a carabiniere," he said. "I helped you because you are a friend."

Il Presidente turned to walk into the kitchen. "You both might want to go down and see this," he said to them. "Pepe has his easel up and wants to do a portrait of all the people at the party. It will be a gift from him to you."

"You go," Nonna Maria said to Captain Murino. "I'll be down in a minute. I want to prepare the pastry platters."

Nonna Maria opened the box of pastries and smiled when she saw the assortment that Minicucci had baked for her—from cannoli to éclairs to cornets to babas dripping with rum. She then turned and opened her refrigerator and took out a large box. She rested the box next to the pastries and slipped it open. Inside was a large cake, the names Paolo and Loretta written across the top. She brought the cake out to the dining room and placed it in the center of the table. She looked up at the portrait of her husband, then turned and saw Loretta standing in the doorway.

"Pepe can't start the painting without you," she said.

Nonna Maria nodded. "My Gabriel and I had a cake made for us that was very much like this one," she said. "I made it for you and the captain myself. I worked from memory, so who knows how it turned out."

Loretta stepped into the room and looked down at the cake. "It's beautiful, Nonna Maria," she said. "And I know it will taste as good as it looks."

"My Gabriel's cousin, Franco, baked that one for us," Nonna Maria said. "As the guests were eating the cake, Gabriel got up to make a toast. It was the only toast I ever heard him make, in public anyway."

"What did he say?" Loretta asked.

"He thanked his cousin for baking the cake and then said that even the most delicious cake lasts for only a few days," Nonna Maria said. "But love, the special love that he had for me and that I had for him, lasts forever."

"And he was right," Loretta said.

"He was," Nonna Maria said. "About the two of us. And I'm right about the two of you."

"Let's take the cake down and share it with everyone," Loretta said.

"The first piece must go to you and the captain," Nonna Maria said.

"And the second piece to you," Loretta said.

Nonna Maria shook her head and smiled. "I never eat sweets," she said. "But you and the captain and the rest of the guests should enjoy the cake."

"Then what will you have?"

"A cold glass of wine," Nonna Maria said. "Maybe two or three, if Pepe takes as long as I think he's going to take painting our portrait."

ACKNOWLEDGMENTS

THIS IS THE third book in the Nonna Maria series, and none of them would have been written if not for the real Nonna Maria. I spent seven glorious summers in her company as a young man and now, through the writing of these books, have been lucky enough to spend even more time with her. She is with me always, through good times and bad, and I am blessed by her presence.

I have been lucky enough to visit Ischia since I was fourteen. I owe so much to so many friends and relatives on that amazing island. To my aunts and uncles—most especially Anna and Ranieri; Nancy and Benny; Francesca and Francesco; Mario; GiovannGuisseppe—who embraced me from our first moments together. To my cousins Giancarlo and Gennaro, and most especially the real Paolo Murino, who helped in so many ways in the writing of these novels. You all have my love.

To my mother, Raffaela, who kept Ischia alive with her many stories during her years living in New York. And to the man who died the year I was born but has still been such a loving part of my life—my Nonno—Gabriel Carcaterra.

I raise a glass of chilled D'Ambra white wine to my friends in

Ischia: Gaspare, Enzo, Branka, Antonio, Christian, Pippo (the best driver in all Italy), Annarella, Angela, Paolo (the Acqua d'Ischia master), Sara d'Ambra, Dario and Ali, Leo, Luisa, Pepe and Salvatore, Alberto and Pepe, John. I hope to see all of you again soon.

Large sections of each novel have been written at Ischia's beautiful Grand Hotel Excelsior, my home away from home, and without the help and generosity of all those who work there, I would be at a loss.

I would like to thank my friends in New York for putting up with my steady stream of phone calls and emails: Hank Gallo, Leah Rozen, Dorothy and Guido Bertucci, Pete and Carol Barry, Captain Joe, Dr. L., Dr. C., PJ, AJ, Alban, Nooch, Anthony Cerbone, Ida Cerbone, Lorenzo Di Bonaventura, Pelham Mary, Larry Zilavy, Qun—next round is on me. And a big thank you to to Dr. David Koslovsky. You are simply the best at what you do.

To the ones who have embraced Nonna Maria from the start, I owe so much more than mere thanks: the truly amazing Kathleen Neville; Meghan Brauer, the director of the Wilson, New York, Community Library, and Marge Clark, the chair—your library is the model for all others to follow. Michael Elia and family and Sevenson Environmental Services for helping to make it all happen, and Michael at the Sunset Grill for his kindness and generosity.

To Christine Freglette of the BookMark Shoppe in Bay Ridge, Brooklyn—you guys never fail to rock the house. To Susan Williamson of Booksy Galore in Pound Ridge, thank you for all you do.

To the Columbus Foundation, thank you for two terrific nights and for all the great charitable work you do. To the amazing Otto Penzler and his great staff at the Mysterious Bookshop—we've been friends forever. And I can never fully tell you how much I value that friendship.

To Adriana Trigiani and Lisa Scottoline—I love you both.

To my editor, Anne Speyer, thank you for helping to put together another book we can both be proud of. And to Carlos Beltran—thanks for the three amazing covers. To my agent, Andrea Blatt, thanks for the care and the hard work. It means a great deal to me. To Lou Pitt, for keeping the car moving forward and always working for me. And to the great Jake Bloom—you will always be the core member of the team.

To the unstoppable Mary Ellen Keating—the best and most caring person I know. To Tim and Tom Keating—thanks for the phone calls and the many laughs. To Rose and Kathy, you know I care about you and it's cool that you love Rocco more.

Speaking of Rocco—my English Bulldog will soon turn two. He has a posse of his own—Angel, Ned, John, Margaert, Jesse, and especially Uncle Safit. He is so very hard not to love. (But Gus remains number one.) A shout-out to Willow (who we miss every day), Siena, George, and Little Henry.

To my children—Kate and Nick—thank you for still caring and loving me the way you do. You both have my heart. And my son-in-law, Clem, who has patiently put together enough of my grandson's toys in the past three years to fill a Home Depot— it's only just begun, my friend.

Finally, to my grandson, Oliver, who will be four by the time this is published: you are the most amazing little man. Your smile lights me up and every moment I spend with you warms my heart. There will be a second grandson by the time this book is in your hands—another boy, name still to be determined. All I know is I'll love him just as much.

Now, on to the next adventure.